JOSHUA

The Group - Week Three

M. D. MEYER

JOSHUA

Copyright © 2011 by M. D. Meyer

All rights reserved. Neither this publication nor any part of this publication may be reproduced or transmitted in any form or by any means, electronic or mechanical, including photocopying, recording or any information storage and retrieval system, without permission in writing from the author.

This is a work of fiction. Names, characters, places and incidents either are the product of the author's imagination or are used fictitiously, and any resemblance to actual persons, living or dead, businesses, companies, events, or locales is entirely coincidental.

Unless otherwise indicated, all Scripture quotations are taken from the Holy Bible, New Life Version. Copyright © 1969, 1976, 1978, 1983, 1986, 1992, 1997. Used by permission of Christian Literature International, P.O. Box 777, Canby, OR 97013.

Scripture quotations marked (KJV) are taken from the Holy Bible, King James Version.

ISBN: 978-1-77069-356-2

Printed in Canada.

Word Alive Press
131 Cordite Road, Winnipeg, MB R3W 1S1
www.wordalivepress.ca

Library and Archives Canada Cataloguing in Publication

Meyer, M. D. (Mary Dorene), 1957-
   Joshua / M.D. Meyer.

(The group ; week 3)
ISBN 978-1-77069-356-2

   I. Title. II. Series: Meyer, M. D. (Mary Dorene), 1957- Group ; week 3.

PS8626.E933J68 2011   C813'.6   C2011-905060-9

Foreword

STEPHANIE NICKEL

If an author leaned over to you at lunch and asked if she could send her unpublished manuscript to you for review, I bet you'd jump at the chance… especially if that author was one of your favorites.

That's what happened to me at the Write! Canada conference last June. What an honour!

Shortly after I returned home, *Joshua* by M.D. Meyer arrived in my inbox. I started reading right away. Having read *Lewis*, another book in the series, it was like returning to Rabbit Lake for a second visit. The characters and setting seemed familiar.

Like most people, I enjoy a nice story with a happy ending. However, too often, novels are too tidy, too idyllic. No matter who we are, we've likely encountered tragedy and heartbreak of some kind. And I, for one, want a work of fiction to authentically reflect the human condition. I want to care about the characters. I even want to experience the whole gamut of emotions.

Wow! What a ride it was reading *Joshua*! One thing's for sure: No-one will accuse M.D. of writing about two-dimensional characters in unrealistic situations. On the contrary, her very believable characters are often in far-too-realistic situations. From Martha, the take charge, faith-filled grandmother to Cynarra, the courageous, heartbroken eight-year-old to Joshua, the lone stallion with a tragic past, readers will come to know and care about each one. And if they're like me, they'll cry, gasp, and even get "the warm fuzzies" on occasion.

A skilled author grabs your attention and keeps you on the edge of your seat as effectively as any movie director and does so without the advantages of a soundtrack, dramatic lighting, and award-winning actors. M. D. Meyer accomplishes this with apparent ease. If you want to dive into a compelling story, I heartily recommend *Joshua*.

Stephanie Nickel reviews books at Book ReVu
www.bookrevu.wordpress.com

"STOP BLAMING YOURSELF FOR A
CRIME YOU DID NOT COMMIT.

God will not hold you responsible for another's sin against you. Satan is the one who would accuse you and make you feel at fault. God is just in all His dealings. You need to have His viewpoint on the matter.

It is sad to see so many commit suicide because of false guilt. Put the shame where it belongs, on the abuser. It is not yours to carry."

Howard Jolly
Moose Factory, 1996

"Come to me, all of you who are tired from carrying heavy loads, and I will give you rest."

Jesus
(Matthew 11:28)

Chapter 1

HER BEST FRIEND... THAT'S how she'd always felt about Joshua. But lately, Missy wondered if she even knew him at all!

Of course, changes were to be expected after all that Joshua had experienced. In the ten years that she had known him, he had gone from a penniless, drug-addicted, suicidal teen to a millionaire property owner and director of a youth program helping troubled teens. The most dramatic change had happened nine months ago when Joshua's friend and mentor, Tom Peters, died and Joshua was willed a large portion of his wealth and the property of Goldrock Lodge.

There had been changes for Missy, too. Tom Peters had been her beloved grandfather and she still missed him every single day. And with her mother's death imminent, Missy and Joshua had been married less than a month after her grandfather's passing.

But perhaps the biggest change for Missy was having her sight restored after being completely blind since she was a baby. Missy still marveled at the technological advances that had made her operation possible—and successful.

Gazing out one of the cathedral-size windows of Goldrock Lodge, Missy delighted in seeing the latest developments as spring unfolded in the Canadian north country. Though it was the third week of April, being north of the 51st parallel, the ice was still on the lake, the sky was an ominous grey and the trees were devoid of leaves. Joshua had gloomed that morning over the weather, saying it was his least favorite time of the year but for Missy, every shade of color painted across her landscape was wonderful, even the dark and grey ones.

Missy tenderly placed her hands on her "baby bump" as her sister, Jasmine, called it. Another change in their lives…

She slowly turned away from the window letting her eyes travel past the large stone fireplace which dominated the south end of the lodge to where Joshua sat hunched at a desk behind the spiral staircase that wound its way up to the second floor of rooms at the back of the lodge.

Joshua didn't turn as she approached, his entire focus on the Income Tax papers that he was working on. It was going to be quite a complicated process this year. The Goldrock Lodge property had been privately owned but was completely surrounded by the Indian Reserve Land of the Rabbit Lake band. Joshua, as an Ojibway, had Indian Status, which in some situations allowed him some tax exemptions but with the newly combined provincial PST and federal GST taxes into one HST tax, things were no longer as simple as they had once been. Goldrock Lodge and the five cabins on the property had for the past winter been home to seven troubled teens and as many full and part-time staff. There had been wages paid but everything was under the umbrella of a non-profit organization.

When Missy reached out her hand to caress his shoulder, Joshua startled and the look he gave her was annoyance that only gradually softened into weariness.

"You're working too hard," Missy said, gently massaging his shoulders.

Joshua shrugged her off. "It hurts when you do that."

Missy sighed. It was a long-standing argument between the two of them. Joshua's neck and shoulder muscles were often a mass of knots. Missy knew a good massage would help him and, according to various other family members, she did know how to give a good neck and shoulder massage.

She leaned forward and wrapped her arms around him, feeling the slight pressure of her swollen belly pressed up against the back of the chair. "You're just so tense."

Joshua gently stroked her arms and then turned in the chair, in the process once more shrugging her off. But his voice was kind and his dark brown eyes gentle as he asked, "Are you feeling any better?"

This was her tenth week in the pregnancy and Missy was used to the question and ready with her answer. "A little," she said, unable to suppress the accompanying sigh.

What others described as "morning sickness" never seemed to really leave her but it did decrease in intensity throughout the day. Today it hadn't been too bad, even though she had only had herbal tea so far and although it was almost noon, she was still in her robe, not feeling well enough to get dressed yet. It was a nice robe, though, made out of white silk, hand-painted with chrysanthemum flowers, a gift from her aunt, Coralee. Missy knew that even on her worst days, the beautiful white robe looked wonderful up against her ebony skin and curly black hair.

"And how are the taxes going?" Missy asked, quickly diverting the topic away from her health.

Joshua shook his head. "Not good—and there are so many interruptions…"

Missy began to move away but he caught at her arm. "Not you," he said gently. "I didn't mean you."

"You've had a lot of phone calls this morning…"

"Yes, and this last one—from the Department of Northern Development and Mines—apparently, someone has registered a complaint implying that there are some safety issues on the old Goldrock Mine site on our property."

"But all the mine shafts were blocked off years ago," Missy protested, "and you keep all the old buildings locked."

"They want us to put fences around the buildings as well," Joshua said, "and some of them need to be torn down, in particular the headframe. They said that it's an eyesore, a 'blot on the pristine wilderness landscape.'"

Missy blinked in amazement. "But it's not. It's a landmark. People can see it as they boat past on the lake or when they're flying over our community. It's—it's a historic landmark. It's important. We can't just tear it down!"

Joshua smiled. "That's how you and I see it."

"And everyone else who lives around here," Missy protested.

Joshua sighed. "Not everyone. Someone local registered the complaint. I—I have a feeling it might have been a family member…"

Missy shook her head in disgust. Probably Yvonne Quill… Joshua's aunt… ever since Joshua had inherited the money and land, she had been trying everything in her power to take it away.

Joshua let his hand drop, releasing the gentle hold he'd had on Missy's arm. He turned away from her and gazed blankly at the papers on the desk before him. "Sometimes," he said, "I wish I had never been given all this."

Missy put her arm around him. "Grandpa wanted you to have it. He knew you would fulfill the dream that you both had. And Joshua… You did it! You did fulfill that dream when you had the youth program here this past winter."

"It was just a test run," Joshua said dispiritedly. "And I don't know how well it went. I know Michael has some concerns…"

Michael… He was her cousin and had always been a good friend, also. But he could be critical and overbearing, more of a leader than a follower. He'd been one of their counselors in the program and he'd done a good job but he seemed to always be questioning Joshua's leadership. And Joshua didn't need anyone or anything else to erode his self-confidence.

Missy was trying to think of something reassuring to say when the sound of tires over crushed rock made them both turn towards the front windows.

And here she was still in her robe… "I'd better get dressed!" she exclaimed. At least Joshua looked up to receiving company. Since becoming owner of Goldrock Lodge, he'd taken special care of his appearance. Even though it was early in the day, he was neatly dressed in a camel-colored, long-sleeve button down shirt, dark brown pants and brown leather loafers.

Missy smiled at her handsome young husband before turning to dash up the stairs to get changed.

THE FRONT DOOR WAS MADE of solid oak and Joshua could barely hear the faint tapping that someone was making on it. Tom Peters hadn't liked the idea of anything electronic and had never even considered installing a doorbell.

Joshua hurried across the large dining area, skirting tables and chairs as he called out, "Coming!"

He pulled open the door to a stranger—a girl who looked to be about seven or eight with an aura of frizzy black hair that accentuated her elfin face and her huge, brown eyes that held more sadness than any child's should. Her clothes were new looking but practical—a purple long-sleeved T-shirt, blue jeans and black running shoes—and a dark green packsack hung heavily from her small shoulders.

Joshua, unable to fathom who she could be, or what she could possibly want, finally managed a hesitant greeting. "Hello…"

"Will you help us?" the little girl asked.

A reasonable enough request if the lodge had been located on a busy highway—but this was the end of the road—a lake on one side and bush and rock on the other. Joshua pulled his eyes away from the child to look at the vehicle parked just behind the lodge's van. The driver had stepped out and was lighting up a cigarette, nonchalantly leaning against the Ford LTD as if the outcome of their conversation was of no consequence to him. Joshua didn't know the man personally but recognized him as someone who hired out his services and vehicle as a taxi when one was needed around the community of Rabbit Lake.

Joshua nodded in greeting to the man before turning questioning eyes back to the little girl.

"He's just someone we hired to drive us here," the girl said dismissively.

Us? Joshua noticed then that there was another passenger in the car. He was hunched over like an old man—or someone who was ill.

"I'm not a doctor," Joshua began. "There's a Health Center back where you came from. You should have turned left from the airport road, not right. Your driver should have known…"

The little girl stamped her foot but the tears that sprang to her eyes spoke more of desperation than impatience. "I don't have time for this! Are you Joshua Quill?"

"Yes, I am," Joshua answered, more bewildered than ever.

"Who is it?" Missy came up behind him.

"I—I don't know," Joshua answered, glancing briefly at Missy before turning his eyes towards the little girl again.

Her desperation had turned to fear. "He said you wouldn't turn us away!" she sobbed. "He said it would be against your religion. He said…"

Missy knelt down and gathered the little girl into her arms. "It's okay," she said, "it's okay."

The child looked over Missy's shoulder and up into Joshua's eyes. "Will you help us?" she pleaded.

"Of course we will," Missy assured her.

Joshua looked towards the car again. Though the old man's head was bowed, there was something vaguely familiar about the set of his shoulders. Then he lifted his head and turned slowly to face Joshua.

"No, we won't."

Missy gasped. "What did you say?"

Joshua reined in his runaway emotions, tore his eyes away from the car and glared down at the girl. "Okay, you can stop that crying now. I will speak to my brother and then you will both go back to wherever it is you came from."

Joshua ignored the look in his wife's eyes—and the child's.

He'd come for money. Or maybe it was just some kind of sick game that he was playing. Bryan was good at that.

Joshua stepped over to the car and wrenched open the door.

Bryan had his head resting on the back of the seat. He looked as if it was taking all his energy just to remain in an upright position. Always on the thin side, Bryan now looked gaunt, the skin stretched tightly over his bones.

As he lifted his eyes towards Joshua, there was a flash of the old insolence, a ghost of the sarcastic smile and then his face fell again and he just looked old and sick and tired. He looked, in fact, as if he were dying.

But Bryan was an actor—had been all his life—even before he'd taken it up professionally and Joshua was unsure whether or not to believe what his eyes were telling him. There was a lot you could do with makeup…

He heard her scream of outrage but was unprepared for the onslaught of fists and feet from the little girl. For someone so small, she knew how to kick and hit pretty hard.

Joshua was too shocked to react but with soothing tones and kind words, Missy pulled the little girl away and gathered her into her arms once more.

Joshua took a deep breath and turned back to face his brother. Bryan smiled sardonically up at him. "Nice wife," he commented in a rasping voice. His eyes traveled to the building behind him. "Nice house."

Joshua felt his jaw tighten. "What do you want?" he demanded.

Bryan's expression softened as he looked at the little girl still weeping in Missy's arms. "Sanctuary," he said.

For the first time in years, Joshua felt like swearing. Bryan had always liked to play with words. The same way that he liked to play with people… toy with their feelings… destroy their lives.

But he wouldn't let him do it—not now. And not ever again.

Joshua turned his attention back to the man who had taxied his brother and the little actress over, presumably from the airport. Must have been a charter, since the last plane into the community had been at 8:30 that morning…

"Take them back to wherever they came from," Joshua ordered.

"Joshua!" Missy cried tearfully.

He looked down at her, still kneeling, holding the child. She had a shocked expression on her face as if she didn't know who he was anymore—as if he was some kind of horrible, heartless monster.

Bryan was the monster—not him! *Didn't she remember what his brothers had done to him—the evil deeds they had perpetrated against him—and so many other young children?*

Of course! Missy had never met Bryan! She didn't know who he was...

"Missy, this is Bryan, one of my brothers."

He watched as the full impact of his words slowly sunk in. She knew what he—and others—had suffered at the hands of his brothers—the physical, sexual and verbal abuse.

Missy released the child and rocked back on her heels, her gaze still fixed on Joshua. "What's going on?" she asked.

He suddenly felt very old and very tired. "I don't know, honey." He shook his head. "I don't know."

The little girl spun around to face him. "We came to you for help and you're turning us away!" she screamed. "That's what's happening!"

Pushing past Joshua, she closed the car door on Bryan's side then ran around to the other side and got in, slamming the door shut behind her.

The taxi driver ground out his cigarette and made a move towards the car.

"Wait!" Joshua called.

The driver stopped and looked down at his watch. "The meter's running," he growled.

Joshua knew there was no meter in the beat up old Ford but he pulled his wallet out and handed the man a couple of twenties. Satisfied, the driver lit up another cigarette and turned his gaze towards the lake.

Missy was on her feet now, conflicting emotions in her eyes. "We could get them settled into a hotel…" she tentatively suggested.

The idea of one of his brothers spending the night in a hotel room with a young child sent shivers up Joshua's spine.

Who was this child? If she was an actress, she was very, very good.

"Joshua…" Missy began again, "I'm cold. Maybe we could all go inside for just a bit—and discuss things there."

There's nothing to discuss!

He felt Missy's arm around him and barely suppressed a sob that rose from deep within. *Invite Bryan into his home?* His gut wrenched at the thought and sweat beaded on his forehead.

"We can make some phone calls… figure out some other arrangements for them…" Missy suggested, her arm still reassuringly around him.

Joshua shuddered then nodded briefly before stepping to the car and pulling open the door on Bryan's side.

Their eyes locked and for an instant, there was that old sardonic gleam in Bryan's eyes. Joshua almost slammed the door shut again but Missy had moved to the other side of the car and in a gentle voice, was inviting the little girl to come inside the house.

"Just until we straighten this out," Joshua cautioned. "It's too cold out here to stand around discussing things."

Raw hatred burned in the child's eyes as she turned away from Missy to glare at Joshua. "We'll find somewhere else to go," she declared.

"No," Bryan said.

Joshua was shocked at the sound of the weak rasp. Could Bryan be faking even this?

"You can come in or go away—I don't care." But the tremble in Joshua's voice betrayed his true feelings.

"He can't walk by himself," the little girl said. "You have to carry him."

Joshua was appalled. "What!" he exclaimed.

Bryan smiled faintly and explained. "I had an attendant. He got me settled into the taxi and then I sent him back on the plane."

So they had really and truly burned their bridges…

Joshua glanced at the smoldering rage in the child's eyes, swallowed back the revulsion he felt and bent into the car to help his brother.

Joshua slid one arm under Bryan's knees and with the other, supported his back. Bryan groaned as he was lifted up and out of the car.

"Be careful!" the little girl cried out.

Joshua glanced down at her. "I will be," he promised.

Joshua averted his gaze from his brother's eyes. He didn't want to see the look of gratitude there.

"You better not hurt him!"

"I won't."

It was like lifting and carrying a bag of bones. Joshua would never have believed that a full-grown man could weigh so little.

And it was obvious that every small movement caused Bryan pain. Joshua tried to walk smoothly, setting each foot down slowly and carefully but it was the way that he was holding his brother that was the biggest problem. He needed to hold him close and use the full length of his arms to support his body. His loose hold meant that Bryan was jostled slightly with each step.

As they walked into the lodge, Joshua glanced quickly around the large front room wondering where he should set Bryan down. The dining room chairs looked too uncomfortable and a bed, or even the couch, seemed too permanent. Maybe one of the easy chairs…

"Bring him to the bathroom," the little girl ordered. "And be careful!"

Joshua was too startled to disobey. As Missy instructed the taxi driver where to set down the bags, Joshua carried Bryan across the dining room and through the kitchen to their guest room which had a large bathroom attached.

The little girl had followed them. "Just put him down on the floor," she told him.

Easier said than done! Though Bryan was very light, he made an awkward load and it was especially difficult for Joshua to set him down on the floor without jarring him further. And he could tell by the groans of pain that he wasn't being very successful at it.

The girl knelt down beside Bryan, slid off her dark green backpack and pulled out a shiny purple case. It looked like something a girl might have to hold her makeup or maybe dolls or something.

The case didn't contain dolls or makeup.

It was filled with medicine.

Joshua stared at the assortment of containers. There were pills, liquids, some ointments and creams, all with clearly marked prescription labels. He was especially shocked to see a syringe but realized that it was the kind used for giving medicine to babies.

"You can go now."

Joshua was startled by the vehemence in her young voice and the cold anger in her eyes.

But maybe he deserved it.

It was becoming increasingly obvious to Joshua that there was no way that even Bryan could fake all this—especially the extreme weight loss.

"Is there anything I can get you?" he asked, edging towards the door. "Anything you need?"

The girl didn't even bother to raise her head again.

Joshua backed out of the room and almost bumped into Missy coming in.

"What happened?" she demanded. "Why is he on the floor?"

"It's okay." The girl's voice was surprisingly gentle when talking to Missy. "There's some things we have to do that are just easier in the bathroom."

Missy knelt down beside them. "What kind of things?" she asked.

But Joshua was not to be included in her answer. The little girl stared up at him with narrowed eyes. Joshua turned quickly and left the room, not stopping until he was through the kitchen and dining room and sitting at his desk again.

He couldn't believe it! It was like he was the bad guy here.

It was not a role he was used to playing. The victim, yes. The survivor, certainly. Even the role of rescuer, helper, teacher, facilitator, leader…

But the role of villain was completely unfamiliar to him.

But of course, Bryan had always been able to mess with his mind.

And now that Joshua had a wife and a child on the way, a home of his own, a ministry with young people… Yes, it made sense that his brother would want to smash and destroy all that Joshua had built up.

He couldn't allow him to do that.

Even if Bryan was sick, that's what hospitals were for…

"Joshua…"

It was like a healing balm to have her hand on his shoulder. Missy's voice was gentle. "I know this must be hard for you."

Joshua nodded his head but didn't look into her eyes. He wasn't sure it was compassion that he wanted or needed just then. *But what did he need?*

"Cynarra and I helped Bryan into bed. She gave him some medicine. She thinks he might sleep a bit now."

"Cynarra—that's her name?"

"Yes," Missy answered, as she rubbed his back in a slow, circular motion.

Joshua turned to face her, feeling irritation rising up within him again. "What's she doing with him anyways?" he demanded. "She's just a little kid. She should be home with her family…"

"He's my father."

Joshua and Missy turned to stare in shock at the little girl walking towards them. She had spoken so matter-of-factly. There was no drama in either her words or her actions.

She just looked tired.

"Here, honey," Missy said gently. "Come sit here on the couch. I'll get you a drink. Would you like a glass of juice? Have you had lunch yet?"

"I—no, it's okay."

Missy smiled kindly. "I'll just make you a quick sandwich," she insisted. "And do you prefer apple or orange juice?"

"Orange, please," the little girl replied politely.

As Missy hurried away, silence fell between the two of them. Joshua walked over to the fireplace and lit a fire in it.

"He couldn't be your father," he said.

She didn't answer him and after a moment, Joshua turned and looked at her.

It was as if she had been waiting for his full attention. She looked back at him with steady eyes and spoke the words slowly and carefully. "I had two fathers till they got divorced. Bryan and Terry had a big fight over who would get me. Bryan won. He has sole custody. He's my only family. There's no one you can send me away to if you don't want me. And I won't leave Bryan. I'm going to stay with him until—"

Her lower lip suddenly began to quiver. She bit down hard on it, took a deep breath and raised her chin. "I'm not ever going to leave him," she said in a shaky but determined voice. "Not ever!"

Chapter 2

CYNARRA STOOD UP AND RAN from the room, almost colliding with Missy on her way towards them with a sandwich and a glass of juice.

The little girl didn't stop but kept going straight into the guest bedroom where her father lay.

Missy set the food down on the kitchen table and followed Cynarra, wondering what Joshua had said this time to upset her so badly.

CYNARRA WAS STANDING WITH her eyes fixed on her father, silently weeping. Missy longed to take the little girl into her arms.

But just then, Bryan opened his eyes, smiled lovingly at his daughter, and weakly raised and lowered his hand on the bed signaling for her to come up beside him.

"But I don't want to jiggle the bed and hurt you, Daddy," Cynarra said, her little child's voice filled with tears.

He shook his head and continued to smile weakly.

Cynarra was very careful as she slowly climbed up onto the bed.

Even so, Missy could see that the slight movement caused Bryan pain. She was suddenly thankful that they had replaced the mattress last year. If it had been the saggy old one that they'd had before…

Missy watched fascinated as Cynarra lay down an arm's length away from her father. Then she very gently placed a hand on each side of his face and he did the same with her.

She was still crying but seemed a little calmer now.

"Cynarra…"

Missy thought she had never heard a name spoken more tenderly.

The little girl watched her father's face intently as he spoke.

"…Don't be afraid."

Missy felt a rush of air past her, a blur of colors before her eyes.

Joshua snatched Cynarra off the bed and thrust her into Missy's arms.

"Get her out of here!" he commanded.

But Missy was too shocked to do more than draw the little child close.

"There'll be none of that in this house!" Joshua spoke in a voice trembling with rage.

Missy stared at him, still unable to move an inch. This couldn't be her husband… this angry, raving madman!

"You might have suckered my wife into believing you but I know you, Bryan Quill. *I know you!* And you're not welcome in my house. If you're sick, you can go to a hospital. But you're not taking this little girl with you. That's all over now. And don't get any ideas of fighting for custody. Or you'll spend your last days rotting in jail—"

Cynarra had wiggled out of Missy's arms and before anyone could stop her, had launched herself towards Joshua.

"Cynarra…" Bryan called in a weak, rasping voice.

She gave Joshua a final kick in the shin before turning back to her father.

"Don't fight them," Bryan said in a fragile voice. "They're going to help us."

"No…"

The deep pain in her voice tore at Missy's heart. "Yes," she said, kneeling down to the little girl's level. Without daring to look up at Joshua, she continued. "We *are* going to help you, Cynarra."

But the hurt and confusion remained in the little girl's eyes. Her voice trembled and there was more fear than malice as she said, "I don't like you."

She turned to look up at Joshua. "I don't like him."

Missy followed her gaze.

Joshua was standing in the doorway as if caught between going and staying. His face was pale and his eyes wide open and staring at the three of them, as if together they represented a speeding Mack truck baring down upon him.

But there was nothing Missy could do to help him. The little girl needed her reassurance. "I promise you…" Cautiously Missy reached out to touch her hand. "I promise that we will help you, Cynarra."

But even young as she was, Cynarra could understand that it wouldn't be that simple. Missy wanted to help. Joshua obviously didn't.

She turned red-rimmed eyes back to her father. "We shouldn't have come here," she said with more resignation than rebellion in her voice.

There was no answer.

His eyes stared vacantly and his pale lips were parted a little.

For one terrifying instant, Missy thought that he had already left them.

Then slowly there came a faint glow of recognition as he focused briefly on his daughter.

"I'm tired," he said. Then he closed his eyes.

Missy felt panic rising up within her once again.

It must have showed on her face. Cynarra spoke softly, "He's only asleep."

Missy watched as Cynarra gently tucked the covers up around him, her actions more like that of a mother than a daughter.

Too young to be so old…

"Hello, anybody home?" a voice called from out in the main room.

Missy's grandmother…

She'd arrived in Rabbit Lake just the day before. And she'd spent the night with her other granddaughter, Jasmine, and her new baby girls.

Missy didn't want to leave Cynarra, even for a minute. She glanced up at Joshua.

He still looked dazed and hurt and confused. Their eyes met for an instant. Then he turned and stumbled out of the room.

Missy forced her attention back to Cynarra. "It's my grandma. Her name is Martha—Martha Peters."

"Is she like you…?" Cynarra asked cautiously. "…And like me?"

Missy hesitated, unsure of what the little girl was asking. "She's nice…"

"But is she Black?" Cynarra whispered.

Missy leaned forward. "Yes, honey, as a matter of fact, she is."

Cynarra nodded wisely. "I thought she might be."

Missy decided that now probably wouldn't be a good time to tell her that she was a granddaughter by adoption, not by birth. If it made Cynarra feel a little more accepted… a little less alone.

"Would you like to meet her?" Missy asked.

Cynarra smiled for the very first time and Missy thought she had never seen such a beautiful smile.

Cautiously, she took the little girl's hand and led her towards the door.

Joshua had made it as far as the first dining room table. Martha must have come the rest of the way to meet him.

Missy stopped in the kitchen doorway, unsure if she should continue. Martha had her arm around Joshua.

Her voice was filled with concern. "But why is he here—and where?"

Joshua raised his head and looked towards the bedroom.

Missy watched the dazed look in his eyes turn to surprise and then defeat as he saw the two of them standing together.

He averted his eyes. "I'm not handling things very well right now."

Martha hadn't seen Missy or Cynarra. She was turned slightly away from the kitchen and all her focus was on Joshua. "Whatever it is," she said. "We'll get through it—together."

Joshua smiled sadly. "You sound like Tom now."

Martha wiped at a tear and then reached for her purse and got out a Kleenex as more tears began to fall.

Joshua quickly apologized. "I'm so sorry," he said.

Martha patted his hand. "No, it's okay, really." She blew her nose and smiled gently as she continued. "I like it when people talk about my Tom. Usually everyone's afraid to mention his name. It's almost as if he never existed or something."

"He was like a dad to me," Joshua said.

"I know he was. And you were like a son to him." Martha dabbed at her eyes again. "He was so proud of you."

Joshua bowed his head. "He wouldn't be today."

Missy wondered if she should go back into the bedroom or at least the kitchen. Maybe Cynarra would eat her lunch now. It was probably doing Joshua some good to be able to talk to Martha.

She tugged gently on Cynarra's hand and turned back into the kitchen.

"You said I could meet her," Cynarra protested.

Missy hesitated but it was too late to leave now anyway. Martha had heard her voice and was rising to greet them.

"Missy, honey, how are you?" Her smile included both of them as she asked, "And who's your young friend?"

"My name is Cynarra Quill." The young girl stepped boldly forward with an outstretched hand.

"Cynarra *Quill*…" Martha glanced at Joshua before taking the small hand and smiling warmly. "Nice to meet you," she said.

But Cynarra didn't miss the brief exchange between Martha and Joshua. She raised her chin a little higher and added, "My father is Bryan Quill."

Martha's smile didn't falter. Though she knew very well who Bryan was and what he and his brothers had done to Joshua, it made no difference in her friendly attitude towards this young child.

"Would you like to join us?" Martha invited. "Have you had lunch yet?"

Missy smiled. Her grandma slipped so easily into the role of hostess.

But Cynarra was looking daggers at Joshua. "I won't sit with *him*."

Martha blinked in surprise. "Now honey," she admonished gently, "what's between your father and your uncle shouldn't affect your relationship with Joshua. You'd be really missing out on something if you didn't get to know your Uncle Joshua. He's—"

"I already know him," Cynarra interrupted. "And I hate him!"

Martha was clearly shocked by the child's outburst.

"But, honey…" she began.

"She's right," Joshua mumbled. "I'll go. You two visit."

But as he stood to his feet, Joshua seemed suddenly disoriented. He looked around the room, his eyes sweeping past Missy as if she wasn't even there.

"Joshua…"

"The taxes…" Joshua spoke as if in a daze. He began walking, focusing on the table where the tax papers were spread out, as if he were shipwrecked and the table was a distant shore to which he must swim.

Missy watched him go, once more torn between her husband's needs and this little girl's needs.

"I've never had a grandma."

Missy noticed a wistful tone in Cynarra's voice.

But she'd certainly said the right thing as far as Martha was concerned.

"Actually…" Martha's eyes twinkled as she looked down at the little girl. "I'm a great-grandmother now."

They both sat down at the table as Martha continued, "I was just down visiting with my two great-granddaughters. They're twins."

Cynarra's face lit up. "Twins!"

"Yes, one's a little bigger than the other right now so I can tell them apart. But when they get older…"

Missy backed away. It all felt so unreal. Bryan was quite possibly dying. Joshua was in some kind of shock. And these two were chatting about babies as if they were just having a nice little visit over a cup of tea.

Tea... She should bring Cynarra the lunch she'd made for her. And she should make her grandma some tea. But maybe she would prefer coffee…

"Their names are Amy and Ashley," Martha continued in a cheery voice.

Missy turned away. She would make tea.

And sandwiches for all of them…

There was already one made for Cynarra. Missy knew her grandmother was health conscious and would prefer rye bread with lettuce and tomato and just a thin slice of cheese. She made the same for herself as well.

Missy often encouraged Joshua to eat more nutritious food but this time, she reached for the white bread and some bologna that Joshua had bought when Missy had been down at the hospital with her sister.

She put butter on both pieces of bread, cut a thick slice of bologna and spread ketchup all over it. She'd never done it before but she'd watched Joshua make it and knew that was how he liked it.

The "pink cow" was a little harder to find. Missy finally located it way at the back of her spice cupboard. This "food" item wasn't one that she usually approved of either. "It's just food coloring and sugar and chemicals," she'd complained to Joshua when he'd put it into their shopping cart several weeks before.

But she knew how much he liked the bright pink, strawberry flavored syrup mixed in with a tall, cold glass of milk.

Missy brought the tea out first and then Cynarra's juice and sandwiches for the three of them.

Martha stopped talking long enough to say thank you but didn't question why Missy wasn't joining them yet. She just poured the tea and kept on visiting with Cynarra.

The little girl was taking to her like a fish to water!

Missy went back to get Joshua's sandwich and drink. She wished there was something else she could give him. But she didn't have any of his favorite cookies. Maybe she'd go to the store later…

He had a pen in his hand and was looking down at the papers but it was obvious that Joshua's thoughts were elsewhere.

He looked surprised to see her and even more surprised by what she'd brought. He peeled back the bread a little, saw the bologna and raised an eyebrow questioningly.

Missy found herself apologizing. "You always complain about my 'fancy' sandwiches. I just thought…" Her voice trailed off as Joshua's frown deepened.

"He has to leave, Missy. If you care about that little girl at all, you need to realize that. They could keep him at the Health Center and she can have supervised visits. Or if he needs specialized care, they can Med-i-vac him out."

Missy felt her cheeks burn hot. He'd misinterpreted her kind, thoughtful gesture—made it into something it wasn't.

"I'd like you to support my decision," Joshua continued quietly. "But even if you don't, it won't change anything. I have to do what's right for the child."

Missy turned and walked away, her thoughts in a turmoil. How did he know what was best for "the child"? He hadn't made any kind of effort to get to know her. And he was ready to kick her father out of the house even though he was so obviously ill.

Missy sat down at the table with Martha and Cynarra but she couldn't imagine eating her sandwich now.

She glanced over at Joshua. His eyes were on the papers again, his sandwich also remaining untouched.

"May I pray?" Martha asked.

"Yes!" Missy felt as if someone had thrown her a lifeline.

Martha smiled at her kindly. "To thank the Lord for our food," she said gently. "But we can pray for Cynarra's dad and…" she glanced over at Joshua, "…for the rest of us as well."

Cynarra stared wide-eyed at them as Missy and Martha bowed their heads to pray.

"Dear Heavenly Father," Martha began, "we thank you for this food. And we thank you for our families. How precious they are to us. And how we miss them when they're gone." Her voice broke and for a moment she didn't speak. Then she continued on in a stronger but still gentle voice, "Cynarra is about to lose someone very precious to her—her father."

Missy almost gasped in surprise. How had Martha known that? She thought the two of them had only been idly chatting but in just that short amount of time, Cynarra must have already told Martha about her father, confirming more than even Joshua and Missy knew yet.

"Please help us through this difficult time," Martha continued to pray. "We ask for your wisdom and your strength for every day and every hour."

"Amen," Missy said fervently.

"Amen," Martha agreed.

Cynarra was still staring at them open-mouthed, and Missy wondered if it was the first time she'd ever seen someone pray.

"Eat your food, child," Martha said kindly.

Cynarra stared down at her sandwich for a moment then she took a small nibble followed by a bigger bite and another and then another.

Missy watched as the little girl finished both halves of her sandwich and drank down the glass of juice.

"Would you like something more to eat?" Missy asked. "Or another drink?"

But suddenly, there was a dull thump followed by a moaning sound.

It had come from the bedroom.

Cynarra was the first to respond, jumping to her feet and running towards her father. Missy and her grandmother hurried after her, and Missy thought she heard Joshua's chair scrape back…

Before they reached the bedroom, the moaning sound had turned to retching.

Bryan was no longer on the bed but on the floor lying in the doorway of the bathroom.

Cynarra ran to kneel beside her father, holding his head up so that he wouldn't choke when he threw up.

Bryan was gasping for breath and his voice was so weak, they could barely hear his words. "I thought—I could—make it—to the—"

He threw up again. It was a small room and the windows were closed. The smell was overwhelming.

Then there was another smell and it was even worse.

Chapter 3

MARTHA, WITH HER YEARS OF nursing experience, just naturally took charge.

"Help me carry him the rest of the way to the bathroom, Joshua."

"No, I'll help you!" Cynarra fiercely declared.

Bryan looked completely overwhelmed and totally exhausted. "Go," was all he could manage to say in a barely audible voice.

Missy, still in the first trimester of her pregnancy, felt nauseated by the odor in the room. She tugged at Cynarra's hand and turned towards the door.

"Go with her," she heard Bryan rasp as Cynarra pulled away.

"No!" Cynarra cried, "I won't leave you!"

There was anger in Bryan's voice this time as he commanded, "Get out!"

Cynarra ran crying from the room, brushing past Missy on her way through the kitchen.

Missy hurried after her as Cynarra ran towards the front door.

But instead of going outside, the little girl huddled up against the wall and sobbed as if her heart would break—or was already broken.

Missy dropped down onto the floor beside her and wrapped her arms around her. There was nothing much she could do or say other than to just hold her as she cried.

Finally the sobs subsided enough for Missy to understand what Cynarra was saying. "He—he's never—ever—yelled at me—before."

An amazing feat for any father!

"Maybe he knew that was the only way that he could get you to leave," Missy said tenderly.

As she smoothed back the hair away from Cynarra's face, she had a sudden thought.

"I could braid your hair…"

Cynarra looked up with tear-filled eyes. "What?" she asked disbelievingly.

"I—I could braid your hair—if you like—sometime…" Missy was afraid that maybe she had said the wrong thing. The little girl's father was dying and here she was talking about hairstyles.

But it seemed to be just what Cynarra needed. A tentative smile began to slowly form. "You know how?" she asked.

"Um-hum." Missy gently pulled a few more strands of wet hair from off Cynarra's face. "You would look very pretty in African braids."

"I used to get it done sometimes… before Daddy got sick."

"Well, I'm not a professional," Missy said, "but my sister, Jasmine, and I used to practice on each other when we were kids." Missy lowered her voice conspiratorially. "I can even do it with my eyes closed."

Cynarra was impressed. "You can?"

"Um-hum. And I can do a lot of other things with my eyes closed too."

"Really?"

Missy smiled. It was good to see the little girl thinking about something besides death and dying, if even for a few minutes.

"Up until about nine months ago," Missy continued, "I was completely blind. I couldn't see a thing. I grew up that way so I learned how to do lots of things without being able to see."

Cynarra was even more impressed. "You were blind! What was it like? Was everything dark?"

Missy leaned back against the wall. "You know, I didn't really think about that. I guess I didn't really know what dark was because I didn't know what light was."

Cynarra leaned against the wall beside Missy. She closed her eyes and then opened them quickly again. "I don't think I'd like to be blind," she said, "not even for a little while."

"It wasn't so bad for me," Missy said thoughtfully, "because I didn't know anything else. But sometimes now…"

She looked down at Cynarra. She didn't want to put another burden on the little girl. She was already carrying such a heavy load. But maybe it would help…

"Sometimes," she said in a quiet voice, "I get nightmares thinking about being blind again."

Cynarra nodded solemnly. "I get nightmares too," she admitted. "Sometimes I dream that my daddy has already died. I wake up really, really scared and I have to get up and check to make sure that he's okay."

Missy smiled tenderly down at her. "You really love your dad, don't you?"

Cynarra could only nod.

No one spoke for a while then Cynarra asked, "Do you have a dad?"

Missy swallowed hard. The pain was still so fresh. "Yes, but he's in jail right now."

If she'd been an adult, Cynarra might have left it like that. But she was a child. "What did he do?" she asked wide-eyed and wondering.

"He stole some drugs," Missy answered quietly. "He was using them to make himself feel better, to forget some bad things that had happened in his life."

"My daddy never did drugs," Cynarra spoke proudly, "…not till he got sick. And I'm always very careful that he takes just the right amounts."

"*You* give him his medicine?" Missy asked, feeling at once admiration and concern that such a small child had such a big responsibility.

Cynarra's chin rose perceptibly. "I'm not as young as I look, you know."

"How—how old are you?" Missy asked cautiously, wondering if she really wanted to know.

The chin rose higher. "I'm going to be eight years old soon."

Missy tried to smile. "That's great," she said. But she couldn't keep the sadness from her voice.

Too young to be so old...

She wondered if Cynarra had ever had a chance to be a child—to just run and play and have fun.

"So what kinds of things do you like to do?" Missy asked.

Cynarra looked suspiciously up at her. "What do you mean?"

"I mean," Missy asked in a gentle voice, "do you like swimming or skating or baseball or maybe doing crafts? Or do you like to play computer games or just hang out with your friends listening to music or something?"

Cynarra lowered her eyes, *looking almost as if she were ashamed!* Missy wished suddenly that she hadn't asked the question. But it was too late. The growing intimacy between them had been shattered. Cynarra stood to her feet, a deep frown on her face. "I don't do any of those things," she said. "They all sound stupid and—and childish!"

Missy sighed as she watched Cynarra running away from her.

Yes, they are childish—*and you are a child.*

She rose slowly to her feet, wondering if Bryan was ready to see his daughter again. Martha was a good nurse and a kind and compassionate woman besides. She was, in fact, exactly what they needed right now.

Missy wasn't anxious to go into the guest bedroom again. There were some ways that she thought she could possibly help Cynarra but physically taking care of her father was not one of them.

Missy didn't have to follow Cynarra into the bedroom; Martha was already ushering the child out, closing the door behind her.

"Joshua…?" Missy inquired. She hadn't seen him come out of the room.

Martha smiled understandingly. "He's fine, dear."

"But…"

Martha put an arm around her. "C'mon, let's go sit over by the fire," she said. "Bryan wanted to talk to his brother for a few minutes."

"Alone!"

"Yes, alone," Martha said in a firm voice. Then as they walked together across the room, she added, "I haven't really had a proper visit with you yet. I've spent most of my time down at the house with Jasmine and the twins."

Under normal circumstances, Missy would have been only too happy to sit and visit with her grandmother.

In the absence of her mother, Martha had helped to raise her for the first three years of her life, and Missy and her grandmother had always been close.

But now, all Missy could think about was Joshua.

What could Bryan possibly have to say to Joshua that couldn't be said in the presence of others?

BUT AT THAT MOMENT, BRYAN wasn't saying anything at all. His eyes were closed and he seemed totally unaware of Joshua's presence.

Joshua stared at his brother, a cacophony of emotions crashing around in his brain, making clear thoughts impossible.

All these years that Bryan had been gone from Rabbit Lake… It had almost been possible to believe that he no longer existed.

Or maybe it was just that Joshua had chosen to put him out of his mind. Because to remember Bryan was to also remember what Bryan had done.

"Having fun?"

Joshua startled. "What!"

Bryan grinned sardonically. "Watching me."

"*I* don't get my kicks from watching people suffer!" Joshua angrily retorted.

Bryan closed his eyes again, his face expressionless.

Joshua shook his head. Bryan had succeeded in making him angry—again! Bryan had been always able to manipulate him—like a dummy on a string.

"So now you've won," Bryan rasped.

Joshua still couldn't keep the anger out of his voice. "Won *what*?" he demanded.

Bryan continued in the same rasping voice that Joshua was getting used to. "You've won everything! Nice wife. Nice house. Good health."

"Didn't think *you'd* want a *nice wife.*"

Bryan raised an eyebrow. "Wouldn't mind yours."

Joshua felt like hitting him. "Thought you were only interested in men—and young children."

Bryan winced as if Joshua had indeed hit him.

Then his eyes closed again. "I never touched her," he said.

For a moment, Joshua thought that Bryan was talking about their younger sister, Rebecca. All Joshua's thoughts had been in the past.

Now, it was like someone had hit the fast-forward button. There was another little girl now—another vulnerable child.

"I don't believe you," Joshua said. "I saw you—just a few minutes ago."

Bryan sighed wearily and opened his eyes. "You still haven't learned the difference between a healthy touch and a hurting one?"

Joshua gritted his teeth. "You shouldn't be touching her at all—period!"

"She's my daughter."

But Joshua could barely hear the words; Bryan's voice had become so weak. His eyes were closed again and he looked as pale as death.

A spark of compassion rose in Joshua's heart but it was immediately smothered by the rage that blazed through his soul. "You can't have her. Do you hear me? I won't let you ruin her life. I'll fight for custody of her. And I'll win. And I'll make sure that she knows what real love is—and what a real family is—"

Joshua stopped. Bryan had such an amused look on his face.

"What's so funny?" Joshua demanded.

But Bryan's smile had already faded and his eyes closed again. This time, he didn't open them as he spoke in a barely audible voice, "I'm tired."

It was a dismissal.

And suddenly, Joshua could no longer bear to be in his brother's presence. He stood up quickly, knocking the chair over as he went.

As he entered the kitchen, the phone was ringing. Joshua grabbed at it. "Hello," he gasped.

The caller sounded disconcerted. "Uh, hello."

"Yes...?" Joshua tried to put some normality into his voice.

But he obviously wasn't succeeding. The person on the phone still sounded hesitant. "Uh, could I speak to Tom Peters please?"

Joshua had handled dozens of similar phone calls. But today, it was too much. *It was just too much!*

He could think of no reply.

"Hello, sir..." the voice sounded in his ear.

"Who is it, Joshua?"

Missy!

She eased the phone out of his hands.

As he stumbled down the hallway and out of the side door, Joshua heard her calm, clear voice. "Yes, he was my grandfather. He passed away last summer. The new owner? Uh, actually, now is probably not a good time..."

Joshua let the door close behind him, shutting out the sound of her voice.

He wished there was somewhere he could go to be alone—truly alone. His favorite spot by the lake was now part of someone's property, the windows of their house overlooking the sandy point where he used to sit for hours and watch the changing moods of the sky and water stretched out for miles around him.

Joshua leaned against the outside wall of the lodge. He could still see the lake from here.

It was a dark gray, reflecting the dark gray of the skies.

And the dark gray in Joshua's heart.

Chapter 4

As Missy hung up the phone, all her thoughts were on Joshua.

She thought she'd heard him go outside.

He probably hadn't taken a coat and it was getting colder now in the late afternoon. Missy grabbed a coat off a hook in the hall leading out the side door.

Suddenly, she heard the sound of retching again.

Her first instinct was to go and help.

But she knew, even as she approached the bedroom, that there was nothing she could do in her present condition.

"Grandma!" she called loudly.

Martha came quickly but Cynarra, younger and faster, reached Missy first.

She ran past her into the room, anxious to help her father. Martha gave Missy a reassuring pat on the arm as she too hurried past her.

Missy wavered a moment, still wishing she could help then backed away as the awful sound of retching came once more.

"You should have given him some of his nausea medicine," Missy heard Cynarra scold. "You should just let me take care of him. I know how."

"Maybe," Martha suggested softly, "we could take care of your daddy together."

Missy went back into the narrow hallway leading to the side door.

Now *she* needed a breath of fresh air!

Joshua turned towards her as she walked out and his eyes immediately filled with concern. "Missy, are you okay?" he asked.

She smiled weakly. "Yeah, or at least I will be in two or three weeks from now. People say the second trimester is usually a lot easier."

Joshua's eyes grew wider. "The baby!"

Missy had to smile. They'd known she was expecting now for over a month but sometimes Joshua forgot. Missy's smile faded. He'd had a lot to deal with lately—too much.

"At least you brought a jacket," he said, fussing around her like an old mother hen, "but you should have put it on."

"I brought it for you..." Missy tried to protest.

But Joshua had already slipped her arms through the sleeves of the old jacket, a legacy of "Goldrock Lodge" when it had been a tourist camp. On the back of the jacket was a screen-print of the lodge with the old mine headframe in the background.

"Come sit down." Joshua gently pulled her down beside him onto the steps that led up to the guestroom patio.

"I'm okay now," Missy assured him.

He put his arm around her and drew her close. Resting her head against his chest, Missy could hear that his heart was still beating fast. She knew how important this baby was to him. He had talked a lot about breaking the generational curses—the sins that had been passed down from father to son for generations. He wanted to raise a healthy child, whole in body, mind, soul and spirit—a child who would always know that he or she was loved.

"The baby and I are both okay," Missy tried to reassure him. "It was just the sound of your brother being sick."

Joshua jumped to his feet, a wild look in his eyes as he tore open the door and rushed inside.

Missy hurried after her husband, following him into the guest bedroom.

He stopped at his brother's bedside and demanded, "What's the matter with you?"

Martha had been changing the sheets on the bed. Bryan was on his side facing the door, close to the edge of the bed while Martha worked on the other side. The sheets were rolled up behind his back and Martha was about to lift him over the rolled sheets to the clean side. Cynarra stood ready to help.

Martha and Cynarra both stopped to stare at Joshua, obviously shocked by his sudden appearance and angry outburst.

But it was as if Bryan had been expecting the question. "AIDS," he said in a weak, barely audible voice.

"AIDS!" Joshua exploded. "You have AIDS!"

He looked around the room as if seeking an ally. "He can't stay here! Missy's pregnant! We're going to have a baby!"

"You never were too swift," Bryan mumbled.

Joshua's harassed gaze fixed on his brother. "What!" he gasped.

"A few bricks short of a load," Bryan continued with a weary smile.

"Joshua," Martha said in a slow and careful voice, "Missy is in no danger."

"You can't get AIDS from casual contact," Cynarra put in disdainfully.

Missy didn't know what to do or say. Her loyalty lay with her husband. But he was so obviously wrong in this case.

She stepped towards him and tentatively put her arm through his. "Maybe we could talk about this alone—out in the kitchen—just the two of us."

She hadn't meant it to sound condescending.

Joshua pulled his arm away, stared at her as if she were a stranger and turned and stumbled towards the door.

Missy looked helplessly around the room, feeling somehow that she should apologize for Joshua. Bryan's cynical smile and Cynarra's angry glare made her hesitate—would an apology be accepted? She had no right to expect that it should.

Martha smiled reassuringly at her and said, "It's okay, dear. We'll be fine here."

Missy nodded, blinked back some tears and turned to go.

Joshua wasn't in the kitchen or the dining area or over by the fire. Missy wondered if maybe he'd gone outside again.

But suddenly, an overwhelming fatigue descended upon her.

She knew she had to rest, for the baby's sake and for her own.

Maybe if she just sat down for a few minutes… and put her feet up… and closed her eyes… just for a few minutes…

OF COURSE, HE KNEW THAT AIDS wasn't contagious with only casual contact. He'd been taught that in school… TV commercials… posters… everywhere...

He'd reacted purely on emotion. He'd been thinking about the baby.

Joshua walked around the camp property, purposely turning his mind to other things …the fence that needed to be built …the buildings that needed to be repaired—or torn down. There was so much to do. Sometimes it seemed overwhelming.

They'd begun the youth program almost before the ink was dry on the property transfer. Now Joshua wondered if maybe he'd just gone too fast on things.

He'd been so anxious to prove to everyone that he wasn't going to use the money and property for himself but instead to fulfill Tom's, and his, dream of a youth program.

But Tom had given the money to him outright with no conditions attached.

Tom had trusted him completely.

It was Joshua himself who had had doubts.

Yes, Joshua thought, that was really the heart of the matter. If he could somehow have had confidence in himself, it wouldn't have been such a big deal what everyone else thought.

He walked across the frozen ground, wandering past some old buildings towards the abandoned mine headframe. He'd been to the top a number of times in his youth. He knew there was a great view from up there.

Now it was padlocked shut. Joshua checked the lock; it was still secure.

There was graffiti on some of the old buildings. That was a constant chore now that Tom was gone—painting over some of the worst of it. There weren't any windows left; all the windows and doors of the old buildings had been boarded shut. Maybe it was time to tear down a few of them. Or maybe burn them down. But it would officially be fire season in a couple of days—he'd have to hurry if he wanted to get anything like that done this spring.

Instead of circling back to the lodge, Joshua turned towards the small row of cabins. They were still in remarkably good condition but did require constant upkeep. Two of them would need new roofs this summer and several steps needed to be replaced.

The ones that had been lived in during the winter were in better shape than the others. There were three of those: a girls' cabin, a boys' cabin and a smaller cabin that had been dubbed the "Honeymoon Cabin" since it was occupied by the newlywed staff, Rosalee and Michael.

It didn't look like anyone was home at their place. Likely, they were both down helping out with the new twins, Ashley and Amy. Though they were Joshua's nieces, he'd barely seen them at all since they'd been born a little over a week before.

He wondered how long it would be before Andrew and Jasmine got married. Probably it wouldn't be long. They seemed to be very much in love and Andrew was certainly committed to being a father to the twins even though they weren't his biologically.

As Joshua turned down towards the lake, he thought about Cynarra. His other two brothers were both in jail. After Bryan was gone, Joshua would be the closest relative to Cynarra and she would become his responsibility. Really, he thought, Cynarra would end up being more Missy's responsibility than his.

She would likely be in school all day…

Joshua realized suddenly that Cynarra should be in school right now! It was only April. She should still have two months of school left.

Instead, it seemed as if she was acting as Bryan's fulltime caregiver. Why hadn't he hired somone? The child should be in school—not playing nurse-maid to a selfish old man!

Joshua felt anger surging up again. But at that exact moment, the clouds parted and suddenly the most beautiful sunset he'd ever seen appeared before his eyes. Colors that defied description spread across the sky, transforming the grayness, even spreading a kind of afterglow on the dark ice.

And in that instant, Joshua was reminded of how much God loved him.

It was like a gentle hand on his shoulder, a whispered word of encouragement, an affirmation, a blessing.

Joshua, smiling for the first time in many hours, sat down on the dock and watched the sun set, all his thoughts now dwelling on the awesomeness of God.

MISSY AWOKE TO THE GOOD smells of supper cooking. She sat up and looked out the window. A few streaks of fading color remained in the sky from what must have been a gorgeous sunset.

Sunset! Missy glanced at her watch and jumped to her feet. *She had slept for two whole hours!*

She hurried out to the kitchen but found it full of people all busy preparing what looked like enough food for a community feast.

Colin Hill, Rabbit Lake's police chief, was busy stirring a large pot filled with spaghetti sauce. Bill Martin, a local pilot, was in the process of draining a huge pot of noodles and Kaitlyn, his daughter, was making a salad. Missy's cousin, Michael and his wife, Rosalee, were cutting up some bannock and Assistant Police Chief Keegan Littledeer and his wife, Randi, were gathering plates and silverware. And Charles Kakegamic, a long-time friend of the family, was sitting with Martha, drinking tea and talking quietly with her.

Michael was the first to notice Missy standing in the doorway.

He grinned at her. "Grandma called us," he explained.

Then everyone was turning towards her, offering their smiles and words of greeting.

"Thought it was time to call in the troops," Martha said in a gentle voice.

Missy couldn't keep the tears from her eyes. "Thanks," she whispered.

"First we'll eat," Martha said, "and then we'll develop some strategies for helping you two."

Missy felt as if a huge weight had been lifted off her shoulders.

The others turned back to their work but Martha came up close to Missy. "Do you know where Joshua is?" she asked quietly.

Missy shook her head. But in that instant, she heard the front door opening and Joshua appeared.

And he was smiling!

His smile grew wider as he came towards the kitchen. With a raised eyebrow, he asked Missy, "Invited a few people to dinner?"

"Actually," Martha spoke up, "that was me."

Charles Kakegamic stepped forward to shake Joshua's hand.

"We were never meant to walk the path alone," he said.

Joshua nodded solemnly. "Sometimes I forget that."

Keegan and Randi moved past them, carrying a tray each, filled with plates and cups and silverware.

"I think the food's about ready," Colin said.

"Noodles are done," Bill piped up.

"Salad's ready," Kaitlyn added.

"Bannock's ready," Rosalee and Michael spoke in unison, then laughed together as they took the two basketfuls out to the dining area.

Everyone seemed to be moving past them, carrying food.

Missy turned towards Martha. "Cynarra?" she inquired.

"I'll check on her," Martha said.

"Bryan?" Joshua spoke in a hoarse whisper.

Martha squeezed his arm gently. "Jamie's with him. She'll eat later."

Missy nodded. Jamie, Bill Martin's wife, was a nurse and would know what to do to help Bryan.

As Joshua and Missy still hesitated, Martha gave them a gentle push towards the dining room. "G'won now!" she said.

It felt so strange—almost as if they were guests in their own home. Martha asked Charles to pray before the meal. And after they'd all had tea and blueberry cheesecake, Charles stood to his feet again.

Though he had been a special friend of the family for many years, Missy was surprised that he seemed now to be taking almost a leadership role.

Missy wondered if it had something to do with the Native culture—maybe he was considered to be an Elder.

But it was her grandma, an African American woman, who was inviting Charles to take this role…

"Tom was my friend," Charles began. "Maybe my best friend—ever since my wife died many, many years ago."

His voice was gentle and undulating, like waves lapping on the shore.

Charles turned towards Martha and spoke kindly, "I know what it is to walk alone."

He smiled at Joshua. "And I know what it is to have good friends."

"Many nights we sat together here by the fire." He waved his hand towards the fireplace. "And many times, Tom and Martha would come to my houseboat and share a cup of tea—and we'd talk."

He smiled and gazed off into the distance as he continued. "Tom and I were so different in so many ways. But in here…" Charles thumped his fingers against his chest and his eyes burned with passion as he looked around the table. "In here…" he pointed to his heart again, "…we were one."

Missy thought maybe Charles was taking it too far.

"We were like two sides of the same coin."

Yes, definitely too far…

"Even though our skin color was different, our cultures were different, even our views on how things should be done were different, I loved him as a brother and I know that he felt the same towards me."

Missy glanced at Joshua. He was looking as uncomfortable as Missy felt. She wondered where Charles was going with what he was saying. Was he yet another person who felt that *he*, rather than Joshua, should have been given Goldrock Lodge? Missy's anxiety rose as Charles continued.

"As you know, I've taken an active interest in all that has happened here over the years since Tom Peters first arrived at Rabbit Lake—over thirty years ago now." Charles waved his hand around the room. "We designed this place together. Tom had the ideas and I made the actual blueprints."

Missy reached under the table to grasp Joshua's hand. She could feel his tension. *Why had Martha invited Charles to speak now of all times—Joshua had enough to deal with already!*

"Tom always had the ideas—the dreams—the visions. Without him, none of this would have been here."

You got that right!

"Tom was a leader. People naturally followed him. He was like a big, wild shaggy buffalo roaring across the plains. We admired him and wanted to be part of his next big plan—no matter how crazy it seemed at first."

Missy smiled in spite of herself. *Yes, that was Grandpa Tom all right!*

"He grew up on the streets of Chicago and he learned to fight just to survive. He ran his home and his business like a military camp… or maybe a street gang…

"Tom commanded respect," Charles continued. "He demanded loyalty and he expected nothing but the best from those he worked with. It took him many years to learn to trust people—and to learn to trust God. It took many years for Tom to trust people enough to ask them for help."

Missy felt Joshua release her hand. She glanced quickly towards him.

He was standing to his feet.

Charles extended his hand and Joshua walked towards him.

Charles put his hands on Joshua's shoulders. He was taller, older, wiser. He smiled kindly down at Joshua.

"You aren't like a shaggy, wild buffalo," he said. "You're a lone stallion." Charles grinned. "There's still a whole herd of us wanting to be a part of your crazy dreams and big plans. We'll follow you as we followed Tom."

Slowly, solemnly, Joshua nodded. "Meegwetch," he said.

Thank you.

Charles and Joshua embraced. Then Joshua turned towards the rest of his friends and family. "Thank you," he said.

Chapter 5

THEY SPENT THE REST OF THE evening huddled together making plans. Joshua couldn't believe what a relief it was to not be shouldering the entire burden alone anymore.

Charles's offer of help was especially significant. He had worked closely with Tom before and knew how to deal with various government organizations such as the Department of Northern Development and Mines. He had also done all Tom's taxes over the years.

"I have a computer program that I use," Charles said. "You just give me the facts and figures and I'll have it done for you in about an hour or two."

Joshua felt as if he'd been thrown a lifeline. "An hour or two?" he asked incredulously. "Are you sure?"

Charles grinned. "Sure, I'm sure!"

Jamie, a registered nurse, was drawing up a round-the-clock schedule of caregivers for Bryan. Part of Joshua still wanted to protest—just send him to a hospital to die! But that was the coward's way out—Joshua knew that.

Colin, Jamie's husband, had taken her place sitting with Bryan. Joshua wondered how he was faring. Colin, as a young boy, had been another of the Quill brothers' victims. Joshua wondered if Colin was going through the same deep struggles as he himself was. Maybe it was easier for Colin to forgive Bryan. Colin was ten years older than Joshua—he'd had more time to work through some of the issues in his life.

"I have some ideas…"

Michael's loud voice pierced through Joshua's thoughts. He turned slowly to face his wife's cousin, trying to focus in on what he was saying.

"When I's workin' with inner-city youth, we did some real cool things that I think might work up here too."

"Yes," Joshua spoke thoughtfully, "I think you mentioned something like that before."

"You mean, *tried* to mention it," Michael retorted.

"I've been… a little busy lately," Joshua said apologetically.

Michael grinned and punched him in the arm. "That's okay, bro. I know you got a lot on your mind."

Joshua smiled wanly in return. "Yeah."

"So my idea…" Michael began to pace around as he spoke.

Joshua sat back and listened.

"Everyone has a dream," Michael said. "But kids sometimes they get all beat down and think they can never do nothin' with their lives."

Joshua nodded. *Yes, he'd been like that.*

"And when you first ask them, they might say something small like wanting to see a major league hockey game or something."

"That'd probably be a big deal to a lot of our kids."

"Yeah, and that's cool. But what if they could dream beyond that—dream about not just seeing but actually playing on a major league hockey team."

Joshua nodded. "Yeah, I see what you mean."

Michael stopped pacing and stood looking down at Joshua. "What was your dream, man?"

Joshua knew the answer to that question without even having to think about it. But when he tried to speak, his voice betrayed him, his words coming out in a choppy, breathless tone. "I wanted to help kids."

Michael grinned. "Yeah, man, and look what you're doing!" He waved his arms around the room.

"And how did this dream come about?" Michael persisted.

"Tom."

Michael snapped his fingers, emphasizing his point. "Right!"

Joshua shook his head. "But most kids will never be given the amount of money and property that was given to me."

Michael's features froze and he seemed to draw into himself for an instant. His eyes swept around the building, taking in the cathedral ceiling, the skylights, the fireplace…

Then he was back, pursuing his point once again. "But wouldn't you have found some way to fulfill your dream even if all that money hadn't come along?"

Joshua thought about it. What would he be doing now if Tom hadn't died?

Pretty much the same thing—only under Tom's leadership.

And if Tom had willed all his property and money to someone else?

Yes, Joshua knew in his heart, he would have found another way to fulfill his dream. It wouldn't have been on the same scale of course…

"I guess I would have done something, somehow," Joshua replied.

Michael nodded his head, knowingly. "You were right when you said Grandpa Tom, though," he added. "The reason that you dared to believe in your dream is because you had someone who cared enough about you to believe that you could do it. Grandpa Tom was a mentor to you. He took a personal interest. He encouraged you to dream big!"

Yes, he had.

"So that's what we need to do for the youth we work with?" Joshua asked.

"Right," Michael agreed. "But it might not just happen all by itself. We need to talk to the kids about mentors—explain it to them—and help them to choose people who are right for them. And on the flip side, we need to encourage people to become mentors to them."

Michael swept his arms around, including the rest of his audience now, appealing to them as well. "Some of these kids have no one—no one at all."

I had no one…

"The people who noticed me…" Joshua began hesitantly, trying to put his thoughts into words. "The ones who tried to help me—Colin and Grandpa Pipe—and then Tom and Martha—they *saved* me." Joshua's voice was breaking again. "I don't know where I'd be if they hadn't cared enough to reach out to me."

Michael snapped his fingers. "Yeah, and see that's my point. Somehow we gotta convey to these kids that we care.

"Now what you'all did last winter, that was cool," Michael continued. "But it was way too structured, if you know what I mean."

Structured?

Joshua must have looked as puzzled as he felt. Michael continued to elaborate on the point. "We didn't have time to build relationship," he said. "We were too busy running from one activity to the other."

But they were always with the same small group of people—weren't they building relationships along the way?

Michael continued on. "And the programs weren't individualized to meet personal needs. For example, all the guys learned how to fix a snowmobile and all the girls learned how to cook. You had parenting classes even for those who weren't parents yet."

Joshua found his voice again. "It's better to be prepared *before* you have the kids," he said.

"Yeah, and that's cool," Michael spoke dismissively. "But ya gotta make sure your audience is with you. You know what I mean?"

"I—I guess so."

"And you need more down time—just hanging loose—sittin' around. You gotta give the kids opportunity to talk, share their feelings and ask questions on a personal level. We can still have the Bible studies all together but maybe don't try to ram it all down their throats. You know, it's a lot better if people ask the questions first before you give them all the answers."

"Whoa—time out!" Missy interjected suddenly.

Joshua looked up in surprise. All his attention had been focused on Michael. He'd forgotten there were others in the room, listening as well.

"Don't you think you're being a bit too critical, Michael?" Missy asked.

Michael shrugged. "Yeah, maybe."

"I appreciate what you're saying, though," Joshua said quickly. "And I'd like to hear more."

Michael smiled and shook Joshua's hand firmly as if making a promise or a business deal.

"We were thinking about leaving," Rosalee said in a quiet voice.

"What!" Joshua looked from one to the other in confusion.

Michael nodded his head. "We thought you weren't open to any new ideas and we were just about to call it quits. Grandma Peters convinced us that we should try one more time to talk to you."

Joshua couldn't believe it. *He'd come that close to losing Michael and Rosalee!*

"I can't do this without you guys." He glanced around at the others. "I need all of you."

Joshua received a big smile from Charles and a nod of affirmation.

"Jamie!" Colin's voice sounded urgent as he called out to her from the kitchen doorway. She hurried towards him, and they disappeared together towards the guest bedroom.

"…Especially now," Joshua whispered. *I need all of you.*

He didn't even want to know what the current crisis with Bryan was. Let Jamie handle it. She was an experienced nurse. She would ask for help if she needed it.

"We should head home soon." Randi's voice broke through his thoughts. "But maybe we could come back tomorrow and talk some more."

Talk some more?

Keegan placed a hand on Joshua's shoulder. "Yeah, I'd like to discuss a few ideas with you as well," he said. "I'm on the early shift tomorrow, but maybe in the evening…"

Joshua felt too stunned to even speak. As he watched them preparing to leave, saying goodbye to the others, Joshua wondered what Keegan wanted to say to him.

And was it possible that he could really have been so close-minded that no one had wanted to voice their opinions to him? He'd never thought of himself as being that way.

A lone stallion... that's what Charles had called him.

"We need to go too," Michael said.

"But we're just a phone call away," Rosalee added with a smile.

It gave Joshua a funny feeling—as if in spite of their kind words, they were all getting into lifeboats and leaving him on a sinking ship.

He shook his thoughts free and stood to see his guests to the door.

Charles and Martha left together, both promising to return the next morning. Bill went in to speak to Jamie then he and Katie left as well.

Colin and Jamie were still in the guest bedroom; Missy and Joshua remained standing alone by the door after everyone else was gone.

Joshua smiled weakly in her direction. He wanted to ask her how she felt about it all. He'd always considered her an equal partner—someone who was working side by side with him.

Suddenly, he wanted to ask her what her dream was.

Then his courage failed him. What if she wanted to do something wild and crazy? Maybe she'd always dreamed of traveling to a third-world country and helping with a mission to blind people or something...

What if she didn't want to do youth ministry at all?

"Joshua..." Missy's gentle voice touched him like a warm caress.

He walked into her open arms. Her hug was reassuring. In fact, exactly what he needed.

"I love you," she whispered.

"I love you, too."

They pulled away from each other with smiles on their faces, turned as one to step forward again and in that instant, caught sight of Cynarra. She was standing still, staring at them.

Joshua was suddenly reminded of her words: *There's no one you can send me away to if you don't want me.*

When Bryan died, this little girl would be totally alone in the world.

"Cynarra…" Missy spoke in the same tender voice that she had used when she'd said Joshua's name.

No, she wouldn't be totally alone in the world.

Joshua smiled at the little girl but received a frown in return.

Well, he supposed that he deserved that.

But suddenly, he wished with all his heart that things could be different. If he could turn back the clock—welcome her with open arms that instant when she'd appeared on his doorstep.

But it had taken him by surprise. And Bryan…

Bryan…

Colin was standing behind Cynarra. He looked pale and shaken.

Missy must have noticed him, too. She walked quickly towards the little girl. "Honey, can I show you where the baby nursery is? We just painted it a few weeks ago. Can you guess what color it is now?"

Missy had taken her hand and was drawing her towards the spiral staircase. "It's a beautiful shade of lilac. I just love that color. I think it's my favorite…"

Joshua walked slowly towards Colin.

"He stopped breathing," Colin whispered when Joshua was beside him in the kitchen.

"What!" Joshua fought to keep his voice low.

"He started again," Colin assured him. "But it was close—so close!"

Joshua fumbled for a chair and dropped into it.

"He doesn't have much time," Colin said in the same hushed voice. "Jamie says that he may just have a few minutes or hours—or he could linger for days. But it'll be soon."

Colin had the shell-shocked look of a bomb-blast survivor.

"He told me he was sorry." Colin's eyes sought Joshua's then he spoke in a trembling whisper, "I told him he was forgiven."

Colin pushed a shaking hand through his hair. "I need to go home," he said. "Sarah's waiting."

Joshua could only nod.

What was there to say?

He heard the front door open and close. Colin had left to go home to Sarah—and his three children.

Joshua wondered where Missy was. Maybe she'd lain down with Cynarra to try to get her to sleep and maybe they'd both fallen asleep in the process.

The day's events were starting to catch up on him, too. Joshua felt bone weary. But the day wasn't over yet—or more accurately, the night wasn't over yet. The nightmare of having his brother come to his house to die—to confess his sins—to be forgiven…

He didn't hear Missy walk in, and her light touch on his shoulder startled him.

"Honey," she said gently, her eyes filled with concern, "maybe you need to get some rest."

"No." Joshua shook his head quickly.

"You're not alone anymore, remember?" Missy chided. "Jamie made up a schedule. Rosalee will be here at midnight—"

"It's not that simple!" Joshua fought to keep the anger from his voice. "He's my brother. He's dying. And we haven't spoken to each other in over eight years."

Tears sprang to Missy's eyes and she wrapped her arms around him.

Joshua clung to her, feeling her love and unconditional acceptance. Then he forced himself to pull away and look up into her eyes. "He's leaving his daughter with us," Joshua continued in a hoarse voice. "And I don't even know if she really is his daughter legally or biologically. I need to talk to him. But I don't want to talk to him…"

Missy didn't say anything but drew him close once again.

Joshua sighed. It felt good to be in her arms.

"Can I at least get you a cup of coffee or something?" she asked after a moment. "Maybe a glass of milk or juice?"

But even that seemed too big of a decision to make right now.

Missy kissed him on the cheek and moved away from him.

Joshua stared at the bedroom door, thinking about his brother.

"I'm not trying to say anything or make you do anything…"

Joshua looked up at Missy in surprise. Then he saw that she'd prepared and set before him the very same kind of sandwich and drink that he had left untouched at noon.

Joshua was smitten with remorse.

His lovely, kind, beautiful wife trying simply to communicate her love for him…

"I haven't really been myself today," he said in an apologetic voice.

Missy raised her eyebrows and smiled broadly. "No kidding!"

Joshua turned towards the food. "Thanks," he said gratefully, "it's my favorite."

She kissed him lightly on the cheek. "Yeah, I know."

He pulled her in for a real kiss. Then with a big grin, he picked up his glass of "pink cow" in one hand and his bologna sandwich in the other.

Missy drank a cup of herbal tea while she watched him eat. Joshua grinned at her between bites and made regular comments about how delicious his sandwich was. His praise was met by smiles from his wife.

After he'd finished, Missy stood to her feet once again. "I thought maybe I'd give Jamie a little break," she said.

Joshua was immediately concerned. "Are you sure you'll be okay?"

Missy nodded. "Just for a little while. And Jamie will be right here if I need her. It should be okay."

Joshua glanced towards the closed guest-room door. He started to stand up. "I should—"

Missy put a hand on his shoulder. "It's okay, really. I want to do this, Josh."

He watched her go, admiring everything about her—but most of all, her courage.

It was a few minutes before Jamie emerged.

Joshua wouldn't have believed it possible, but Jamie looked even *more* pale and shaken than her brother had.

Joshua felt his heart leap into his throat. *Maybe Bryan was gone for sure this time.*

"Jamie..."

She looked through glazed eyes at Joshua as if he were a complete stranger. Then she slumped down into a chair, put her head in her hands, and began to weep.

She hadn't even known Bryan, had she?

Joshua did a quick calculation of their age differences. Jamie would be about three years older than Bryan. And they had both lived on the Reserve all of their growing up years…

Joshua waited until her tears had subsided a little before speaking gently, "I'm sorry, Jamie. I didn't realize that you knew him that well."

Jamie sighed deeply and raised her head. She looked weary beyond words as she stared at him through red-rimmed eyes.

"I only know him because of Colin," she said in a voice still thick with tears.

"But…"

"Why are *you* here?" Jamie suddenly demanded.

Coming on top of his discussion with Michael, the question drove deep like a knife. "This is my home—and ministry…"

Jamie shook her head and looked desperately around her. "No, no, that's not what I meant. Why isn't Bill here? I need to talk to Bill—or Colin—or…"

"…Or me," Joshua finished in a gentle voice. "Bryan is my brother. Jamie, please tell me what happened."

Joshua waited anxiously as tears began to stream down Jamie's cheeks once again.

"Colin told me that he'd stopped breathing once…" Joshua prompted.

Jamie bowed her head. "No, he's okay now."

"Then what?" Joshua asked gently.

Jamie lifted her eyes, searching Joshua's face for a moment. "I can't forgive him," she finally whispered.

Jamie! Yet another victim?

"…For what he did to Colin."

Joshua's heart rate slowly returned to normal. "Oh, Colin."

Jamie heard the relief in his voice and anger flared in hers. "He still has night terrors! He's 34 years old, he's married, has three children, is police chief and a respected member of our community but he still wakes up crying like a baby in the middle of the night."

So do I.

"I know he's your brother," Jamie continued her tirade, "but Colin is *my* brother and I've watched him struggling all these years to overcome the effects of the abuse he suffered at the hands of *your* three older brothers—"

"It happened before I was born."

Jamie's hand flew to her mouth. "I didn't mean to imply…" she began.

Joshua shook his head and lowered his eyes. He hated being lumped together with his older brothers—half brothers actually. It was almost as if they were from a different family. Bryan, the youngest, was fourteen years older than him. They'd had the same father but different mothers. Joshua's mother had been Amos Quill's second, and his last, wife.

Joshua had been four years old when he'd witnessed the fight between his mother and father—a fight that ended in his mother's death.

After that, he'd been *so* vulnerable—so easily taken advantage of…

Something of what he was thinking and feeling must have reached Jamie. When next she spoke, her voice was gentle. "Sometimes I forget that they mistreated you as well."

Joshua felt his throat almost close up as he glanced towards her and turned quickly away.

"Yes, they mistreated me as well."

Chapter 6

THEY SAT IN SILENCE FOR A few more minutes before Joshua realized that he was staring at his empty plate.

"Uh, would you like a sandwich or something?" he asked.

Jamie shook her head. "Maybe later."

Joshua shoved the empty plate away. Now he was staring at the bare table…

"Maybe it's easier for the actual victims…" Jamie began.

Joshua stared at her. *"What?"*

"Colin was able to forgive him," Jamie explained. "Maybe it's harder for the family of the victim."

It was a new thought—one he couldn't quite wrap his brain around.

Easier for the victim?

"I—I guess you'd have to ask Missy…" He stood to his feet. "I should go and take her place. It's hard for her to be in there. She's had a queasy stomach ever since…"

He had been moving towards the door even as he spoke. His voice trailed off and he didn't look back at Jamie as he quietly opened the door and stepped into the guestroom… his brother's sickroom… his brother's deathbed.

Bryan was watching him as he approached.

In an instant, Joshua's walls of defense crumbled and a tidal wave of emotion swept over him. "Why are you here?" he demanded hoarsely.

There was none of the former sarcasm in Bryan's voice this time—just weariness and sadness. "Cynarra."

"So you're not here for death-bed confessions?"

Joshua heard Missy gasp at the cruelty in his words and in his voice. Joshua felt a similar reaction from the Holy Spirit within him. But he was in no mood to repent. Long suppressed anger was finally being unleashed and Joshua didn't care right now who got hurt in the process.

"Only as requested," came the sardonic reply.

Bryan's answer only fueled Joshua's anger. And something else... *grief?*

He was actually trembling—and he knew it wasn't cold in this little room.

And he couldn't keep the tears from flowing down his cheeks. He swiped at them but more came and still more...

"I would have done anything for you," he said in a tightly controlled voice.

He wouldn't cry! He wouldn't!

"I'm sorry," Bryan said, his voice weak but calm and steady.

"I knew I couldn't trust the others..." Joshua gave up trying to stop the tears and he could do nothing to keep his chest from heaving and his voice from sounding as if he were drowning. "I always believed you. I always, always believed you."

"Will you forgive me?" Bryan asked.

"I always thought that you would have stopped them if you could have. But it was your idea all along, wasn't it? *Wasn't it?*"

"Theirs and mine," Bryan answered.

"I wouldn't have gone with you if I knew they were waiting for me. You always acted so surprised—as if you hadn't planned it all!"

"We planned it together."

"And you watched—you *always* watched!"

"I'm not a violent man."

Joshua turned away and almost fell over a chair. Blinded by tears, his limbs trembling, he sank heavily down into it.

"Your *non-violence…*" Joshua took a breath and steadied his voice. "Your non-violence cut deeper than any knife and bruised more than all the blows I have *ever* received."

Bryan was silent for a moment before continuing in the same quiet, calm voice he had maintained throughout the conversation. "I can't change what happened."

Joshua found himself losing control again. "*I know that!* But would you?" he rasped. "Would you change it if you could? That's all I'm asking."

"I would change it if I could." Bryan bowed his head and his voice grew even quieter. "I would change everything about my life." Then he raised his eyes quickly and spoke with sudden passion, "Except for Cynarra. I wouldn't change her."

Joshua eyed his brother. There was no doubting his sincerity. It was Joshua's turn to apologize. "I'm sorry that I didn't make her feel more welcome."

Bryan smiled wryly. "You'll have lots of time—" His voice broke off suddenly like a lit match blown out by a strong wind.

His eyes closed and his breathing became shallow—*or had it stopped?*

Joshua felt more than saw Missy rushing past him. A moment later, Jamie was at Bryan's side, feeling his pulse, watching for his breath…

She turned after a moment and said in a quiet voice, "He's still with us." She glanced quickly at Missy and then back to Joshua. "I can stay with him now if you like. You both should try to get some rest."

"No." Joshua was suddenly very sure of what he wanted to do. "I'll stay. You can go home, Jamie."

"How about if I stay and you all go get some sleep?" a cheery voice inquired.

Rosalee! Could it be midnight already?

Joshua thanked her for coming but let her know that he really did want to spend time with his brother and that he would call her if she was needed.

Rosalee was quick to oblige either way and Jamie was simply too worn out to protest.

It was Missy who didn't want to leave Joshua alone.

"I really think you should get some rest," he told her, "...for our baby."

Still she hesitated.

"And if you could check on Cynarra again..." he said, taking her hand in his. "I'd like her to have a good night's sleep, too."

Missy bent down, kissed him affectionately, and finally agreed to go. But not before exacting from him the same promise that Jamie had—that he would call for help the instant that he needed it.

He felt her absence keenly after she was gone. It suddenly seemed too quiet, too still. Time passed slowly. Joshua's eyelids began to grow heavy.

"I hope you take better care of her than you did Becca."

Bryan's words shocked him fully awake again.

Becca... Joshua's younger sister... Bryan's half-sister.

Joshua's face grew hot. No one had ever before accused him of neglecting his sister. His grief had been so overwhelming that no one had wanted to add to it by blaming him in any way. But he'd carried the shame and the blame all these years…

"It wasn't my fault," he protested—but *knew* in his heart that it was.

Bryan sneered. "You were there living in the same house and you didn't notice anything?"

Had he? *Had he?*

The question had haunted him for years.

He'd been a child himself. He was only four years older than Rebecca and he'd tried to protect her ever since she was born.

He'd saved her often from his father's fists, taking the blows upon himself instead. He'd protected her from the bullies at school and warned her repeatedly to stay away from her older brothers.

"I tried…" he whispered aloud.

"You'd better do more than *try* with my daughter."

Joshua closed his eyes, wishing he could shut out the images in his head. He'd been the first one to find Becca. He'd actually been in the house with her when it had happened. She'd been in her room… When had she taken the gun in there with her? He should have noticed it missing from its place on the wall… But his father could have taken it… Or one of his brothers borrowed it…

"You should have known!"

Bryan's words pierced like a knife through the still unhealed wound.

Joshua bowed his head, crushed by the pain… past and present.

He *had* failed to protect Rebecca. And would he do any better protecting Cynarra? *He'd certainly got off to a great start!* He'd probably been the one who had hurt her the most since she'd arrived!

Bryan was right to question his ability to care for his daughter. As people were questioning his ability to run a program for troubled youth.

How crazy was it to think that he could help other people's kids when he hadn't even been able to help his own family.

None of them.

His mother had been killed. His father and sister had committed suicide. His two oldest brothers were in prison. And his youngest brother was dying of AIDS.

He alone had grabbed onto a piece of the crushed and broken boat… and somehow floated safely ashore.

No, that wasn't right. There hadn't been anything at all to hang onto. Nothing at all left of the shipwreck that could have been a home and a family. He would have surely sunk beneath the waves if there hadn't been other people who had reached out to him. Reached out to him again and again as he had floundered.

"She won't be alone…" Joshua began to say.

But Bryan had his eyes closed, his breathing shallow once more.

"She'll never be alone." Joshua whispered the words as a vow. "And even if I fail, there'll be others. It won't be like it was for you and me. That's all over now, Bryan."

Joshua didn't know if his brother could hear him or not. But the words had to be said—out loud. The words of light spoken into the darkness that had been pulsating through the room, threatening to engulf them both.

"She won't be alone because I belong to Jesus. He's the one who promised never to leave us nor forsake us. He will be with us to the end of the world. And because of His death on the cross—His shed blood—I am now part of the family of God. I have a whole bunch of brothers and sisters now who love and take care of each other. I'll never be alone again. And neither will Cynarra. If I don't have a chance to introduce her to Jesus, then my wife will or Colin or Sarah will…"

"Talking to yourself, little brother?"

Joshua's face grew hot with embarrassment but Bryan's voice held more sadness than sarcasm. "Could you lift me up a little higher?" he asked with his next breath.

Joshua stood quickly to his feet but hesitated a fraction of a moment above his brother.

The hesitation didn't go unnoticed but the flicker of pain in Bryan's eyes was quickly replaced by a sardonic smile.

"Such a small thing to ask," he said.

Compelled by shame now, more than love, Joshua put his arms around his brother and eased his head and shoulders up a little higher onto the pillows. It was the closest thing to a hug that they had ever experienced.

Bryan's eyes remained closed for a moment. Joshua knew that even though he had been gentle, it had hurt Bryan to be moved. But he was able to breathe a little better now that his head and shoulders were higher.

Joshua straightened the covers around him.

"Some people say that Jesus was a homosexual."

Joshua recoiled as if he'd been struck.

"Of course, I don't necessarily believe that myself."

Joshua eased back down into the chair, somehow swallowing the angry retort on his lips.

"You think I'm headed straight for hell?" Bryan asked, his voice still playful even as he spoke such serious words.

And in that instant, Joshua was suddenly aware that his brother was truly seeking for answers at this eleventh hour of his life.

"That's between you and God," he answered carefully.

"Well, isn't that what your Christian Bible says?" Bryan demanded.

"Actually…" Joshua leaned forward a little. "It says that we're all headed straight for hell."

"*What!*"

It was Joshua's turn to grin. He shrugged his shoulders. "I didn't write the book."

Bryan's eyes narrowed and his nostrils flared. "I don't know what you're playing at but I do know it's written in there somewhere. I've had it read to me enough by people like you. The Bible does say that homosexuals can't be Christians."

"Yes and neither can the greedy," Joshua returned, "and neither can the people who slander one another. That's in that same part of the book that you probably had quoted at you. And I know some really fat Christians and you'd better believe I know some who know how to hurt each other with their words!"

Bryan grew very still again. Not even his eyes moved.

No, dear God! Not now—not when he was so close!

But as Joshua continued to anxiously watch and wait, Bryan's eyes slowly refocused on his. Joshua sighed in relief and whispered a prayer of thanks to God.

"I want to know," Bryan said in an earnest voice.

Joshua got a New Life Version of the Bible down from a bookshelf above the desk and opened it to the book called "1 Corinthians." Slowly and carefully, he read from the sixth chapter, verses 9 through 14:

"Do you not know that sinful men will have no place in the holy nation of God? Do not be fooled. A person who does sex sins, or who worships false gods, or who is not faithful in marriage, or men who act like women, or people who do sex sins with their own sex, will have no place in the holy nation of God.

"Also those who steal, or those who always want to get more of everything or who say bad things about others, or take things that are not theirs, will have no place in the holy nation of God.

"Some of you were like that. But now your sins are washed away. You were set apart for God-like living to do His work. You were made right with God through our Lord Jesus Christ by the Spirit of our God.

"I am allowed to do all things, but not everything is good for me to do! Even if I am free to do all things, I will not do them if I think it would be hard for me to stop when I know I should.

"Food was meant for the stomach. The stomach needs food, but God will bring to an end both food and the stomach. The body was not meant for sex sins. It was meant to work for the Lord. The Lord is for our body.

"God raised the Lord from death. He will raise us from death by His power also."

Bryan had his eyes closed again.

But Joshua knew to wait.

It was a full minute or perhaps two before Bryan opened his eyes again. "I want that," he said softly.

Joshua felt as if his heart would leap out of his chest! He could never have possibly imagined that anything Bryan could ever say would bring him such an avalanche of joy.

"You do?" he breathed.

The sardonic smile was back but Bryan's eyes spoke the truth. "Yeah, and you'd better be quick about it. I'm a dying man, you know."

Joshua smiled too, feeling an accompanying burst of joy. It was the first time in his life when he had actually shared an honest heart-felt smile with his brother.

"I think you already have chosen," Joshua said in a gentle voice.

Bryan raised an eyebrow but conceded. "Perhaps you're right."

"It's a simple act of faith," Joshua said.

"No incantations or incense waved in my face?" Bryan quipped. "Shouldn't I at least be on my knees or in church somewhere?"

"There are no magical words," Joshua said, "and there is absolutely nothing *we* can do to make ourselves part of the family of God. Jesus has done all there is to do. It's a free gift—grace—God's unmerited favor."

"A gift…" Bryan whispered.

"So many people reject His gift—reject Jesus."

"But shouldn't I pray or something?" Bryan asked uncertainly.

Joshua smiled. "You can talk to God anytime—anywhere—alone or with someone else. Jesus has made the way for you. He paid the price for all of our sins. He took the death penalty for us so that we can go free."

Once again, Bryan's eyes closed.

Joshua waited but they didn't open again.

He watched and waited and finally there was a slight movement—Bryan's left eyelid fluttered. Joshua once again breathed a sigh of relief.

He leaned back in the chair and watched his brother. Was it really possible that Bryan was also now his brother in the Lord?

It was so hard to detect any movement of any kind. Bryan's mouth was slightly open, his jaw slack. His eyes stayed closed and it was easy to believe that he was already gone. Joshua wondered if he was "hanging on," as he'd heard that people sometimes did if they had "unfinished business"—especially of a personal nature.

Joshua thought about Cynarra. But surely they'd had time to say goodbye. But then again, Cynarra didn't seem at all reconciled to her father's death. Maybe she knew but couldn't face the awful truth.

There was no doubt that she loved him. Joshua couldn't ever remember witnessing such fierce loyalty. But if he was all she had…

Bryan shouldn't have isolated her to that degree! She should have had friends and family…

But there had been that divorce… And perhaps there had been other friends or family lost in the separation. And it was likely that Bryan had to move often because of his acting career. But had no one cared enough to stick by them? What of Cynarra's birth mother? There had to be someone!

"Bryan…" Joshua whispered into the stillness. "What about Cynarra? You have to tell me about her mother!"

Slowly, wearily, Bryan's eyes opened again. "She has no mother," he rasped. "She has no one."

"But why?" Joshua demanded. "How could you isolate her in that way? She should have had friends and family!"

"We had friends—lots of them," Bryan mused. "Always milling around the successful Native actor and his cute little daughter from Barbados."

"Barbados?"

"We—Terry and I—we paid two women—"

"Paid! Two of them?"

"Yeah, two of them," Bryan said, his tone more defiant now. "They were happy with the deal. They got to keep one of the babies and we got to keep the other. And since they did all the work, once the embryos were implanted, Terry and I paid for them to spend the next eight months in Meta's home country of Barbados. They came back in time for the babies to be born as Canadian citizens."

The long speech had exhausted Bryan and he grew suddenly still once more.

Joshua was grateful. He needed the space to take in all that Bryan had said to him. Her birth mother must have been part of a lesbian relationship and she had become pregnant through artificial insemination. But what still remained unclear was the identity of the father. Surely they must know whose sperm impregnated which woman?

"Are you really Cynarra's father?" Joshua demanded.

Bryan seemed to come from far, far away this time, as if fighting his way back from the very door of death. "It was my sperm," he said wearily, "that united with Meta's egg."

"Meta..."

"Don't try to find her..." Bryan's voice trailed off again. Then as Joshua waited, he began again. "Part of the circle of friends... we chose to avoid... afterwards. We agreed among the four of us that we would have no further contact between the couples."

"But legally..." Joshua pressed.

Bryan smiled. "Legally... she'll be yours soon... if you want her..."

"We'll need papers, documents..." Joshua spoke urgently.

But Bryan was gone again.

Joshua called his name over and over, barely resisting the urge to shake him.

Joshua waited impatiently and finally—*finally!*—Bryan opened his eyes again.

"As soon… as… I go… call my… lawyer…"

"But I don't know…" Joshua began.

"Missy… has… number."

Bryan's eyes pleaded now. "Let… me… go…"

Tears sprang to Joshua's eyes. "No, you can't! Not now. Not yet!"

Bryan smiled faintly. "We'll… have… time…"

In heaven… He was talking about heaven!

"You… and… me… and… Jesus…"

The smile remained on his face. His eyes were still open.

But Joshua knew that his brother was gone—gone to be with Jesus.

He would never ever have imagined that he would cry when his brother died. He had always thought that he wouldn't care or would perhaps even be in some way glad—or at least relieved.

But he wasn't glad and he wasn't relieved.

Joshua fell to his knees by the bed and cried great heaving sobs.

And in that instant, he realized that he'd always loved his brother and had always, *always* wanted the kind of relationship they'd had in this final hour of his life.

We'll have time…

Bryan's last words echoed in Joshua's heart.

We'll have time… You and me and Jesus…

Chapter 7

JOSHUA KNEW HE HAD TO FIND Missy first—and then Cynarra.

He found them both together.

The nursery still had a set of bunk beds in it but they had been shoved over to the far wall to make room for the crib and a rocking chair and shelves full of toys. Cynarra was in the bottom bunk and Missy had pulled some blankets off the top bunk and was on the floor beside her. It looked as if both of them had just fallen asleep with their clothes on, not bothering to change.

Joshua hated the thought of waking them. He wished they could have at least gotten this one good night's sleep. But when Joshua looked down at his watch, he was surprised to see that it was already almost seven o'clock in the morning! He should have noticed the change in light coming in through the windows but all his thoughts had been on Bryan. Time had lost its meaning. Had Bryan and Cynarra only arrived just yesterday?

Just yesterday…

Just a lifetime ago…

Cynarra startled suddenly awake and when she saw Joshua, her face froze into an angry glare.

Joshua knew he couldn't face her grief alone. He knelt quickly beside Missy and spoke her name.

Missy smiled up at him, saw the devastation on his face and became instantly concerned. "Joshua… What is it?" She sat up quickly and took both of his hands in hers.

"Bry-an…" Joshua's voice broke on the syllable. An awful ache remained in his heart.

"Nooo!" Cynarra screamed.

She leapt from the bed and ran from the room still crying, "No! No! No!"

Joshua and Missy quickly followed her down the stairs.

Cynarra ran straight for her father's room but stopped just inches from the bed.

It was as if she knew, without speaking a word—without touching him—that he was gone from her forever.

She began to sway a little and Joshua rushed forward, afraid that she might be on the verge of collapse.

But she heard him coming and spun around with a look of hatred in her eyes that stopped him cold.

Her frozen lips barely moved. "You killed him," she said.

"No!" Joshua gasped. "No, I didn't. Please believe me. I wanted him to live longer. I wanted…"

Joshua's voice trailed off as he fumbled for a chair to sit down on.

"You killed him," Cynarra repeated.

Missy stepped forward. "Joshua didn't kill your father, honey."

But Cynarra's eyes continued to blaze with fury and all of it was directed towards him. Joshua felt its force like a strong wind blowing over the winter's ice.

"Cynarra…" Missy said gently.

"He wouldn't have left me—" Tears sprang to Cynarra's eyes and her voice broke on a high note of pain. "– Without saying goodbye."

Missy tried to put her arms around the little girl but Cynarra pushed her away and ran out the door.

Missy exchanged a quick worried glance with Joshua, and ran after her.

Joshua was once again left alone.

He wondered if there was something he should do. Close his brother's eyes maybe or pull the sheet over his head…

There were surely things that needed to be done.

But all Joshua's thoughts felt confused. And tumbling together and running through them all was the constant refrain, *"You killed him! You killed him!"*

He hadn't of course—but he *had* in Cynarra's mind—and that thought alone was deeply troubling to him.

"She's okay."

Joshua felt Missy's hand warm on his shoulder.

"I brought her a coat. She's just sitting down on the dock."

Joshua jumped to his feet. *"The dock!"*

He was out of the bedroom and halfway to the front door when Missy's words finally sunk in: "She's okay, Josh. She's okay!"

He turned to face her. "But the dock…" he protested.

"She seemed okay," Missy said again.

Joshua rushed to look through the nearest window. He could see her there, a tiny lone figure huddled against the wind, facing the wide expanse of thin, dark ice. It was another chilly, cloudy, spring morning.

"But she'll be cold out there," Joshua persisted.

"I brought her a coat—a warm one," Missy assured him. "She might just need a little bit of time alone. Her father was her whole world."

"Yes, I know," Joshua said sadly.

Then he remembered. Bryan had asked that they call his lawyer right away. He would have the legal papers and documents for Cynarra—and perhaps Bryan's requests for his funeral and burial.

"Bryan gave you a phone number…" Joshua began hesitantly.

"Yes," Missy said, "it's in the bedroom."

As they walked back in there together, Joshua suddenly felt as if he were intruding somehow.

"It's here on the bedside table," Missy whispered.

Joshua looked down at his brother's body. "I don't know what to do," he said in the same hushed tones. "Who do we call first? Should I at least cover his face?"

But it didn't feel right to do even that…

"I'll call Grandma," Missy said softly. "She'll know what to do."

They went together back into the kitchen to use the phone. Missy called Martha first and then Joshua called Bryan's lawyer.

Surprisingly, he answered on the first ring, and it was obviously his home phone number. "Finley residence," came the crisp greeting.

"Hello," Joshua began hesitantly, "I'm sorry to bother you on a Saturday morning…"

"Yes?"

"I am—I mean I was—uh—Bryan Quill's brother."

There was a brief silence on the other line and Joshua worried that maybe he'd gotten the wrong number.

But when Robin Finley spoke again, it was obvious that he not only knew Bryan's name but was also deeply grieved by his passing.

"He didn't think it would be so soon."

I didn't either.

"Did he have a chance to finish… his business?" Robin asked.

"I think so." Joshua hesitated. "Cynarra—"

But Robin quickly interjected. "I have something for her—from Bryan. It's a video. I think it will help Cynarra with—with saying goodbye."

Joshua felt surprise and immeasurable relief and gratitude towards Bryan for thinking about his daughter in this way. Cynarra hadn't had a chance to say goodbye. Joshua hoped and prayed that the video would be of help to her.

"Is she with you now?" Robin asked.

"She's just outside," Joshua answered, looking to Missy for confirmation.

Missy nodded and mouthed: *She's okay.*

"Is she *staying* with you?" Robin asked pointedly.

Joshua hesitated. "She—doesn't seem to like us much. It's my fault…"

"Well, we can't force her to stay with you," Robin replied brusquely. "There are, of course, other options—foster care, etc."

"No!" Joshua took a deep breath and focused on speaking calmly. "No. I promised Bryan I would take care of her. She's my niece. We'll—we'll work something out."

"Good." Robin spoke crisply. "Now, with regards to the body…"

"Yes?"

"Have you done anything yet?"

"No," Joshua replied weakly.

"Good. Did you record the time of death?"

"I—no," Joshua's mind raced. "But it was before seven…"

"See if you can narrow it down. And we'll need a doctor to sign the death certificate. Is there a doctor currently in your community?"

"Yes, I think so."

Joshua heard someone at the front door and a moment later Martha and Charles were by his side.

Martha patted Joshua's hand and began to walk towards the bedroom.

"Don't do anything yet!" Joshua called out to her.

Martha turned around, a surprised look on her face. "What?"

"The body…" Joshua swallowed hard. "Don't—don't do anything yet."

Martha walked slowly back towards him. "Why?"

Joshua repeated her question into the phone. "Why?"

Robin took a deep breath and began, "Bryan wanted his body donated to research—specifically AIDS research. There'll be a charter plane arriving at your airport within the next hour. There'll be attendants on the plane who will remove the body. We'll need a signed death certificate—"

"But what about the funeral?" Joshua interjected. "At least for Cynarra…"

"That's part of the reason that Bryan made a video for her. Perhaps, if she approves, other family members could also watch parts or all of it with her. You could, of course, have your own memorial service at any time you choose."

"But—" Joshua began to protest.

"Listen, I'm sorry, but I need to set things in motion here. Try not to worry. I'll see you in an hour or so."

He rang off before Joshua could speak again.

"Who was that?" Martha demanded.

Joshua sank down into a kitchen chair. "Bryan's lawyer."

"You called his lawyer—*already!*"

"It was Bryan's request that we call him right away," Missy said.

Martha turned back to Joshua. "And…?" she prompted.

Carefully, Joshua began to explain all the details of his conversation with Robin. Slowly, each of the others sank down into chairs beside him.

"He seems to have had everything worked out," Martha commented.

Joshua sighed. "He had a lot of time to think about it."

"So—so we just shut the door and wait?" Missy asked anxiously.

"Not quite," Joshua replied. "Robin said that we need a doctor—to confirm…" His voice trailed off.

There was no need in Joshua's mind to confirm Bryan's death. He knew the instant that Bryan had gone to be with the Lord.

"And the time…" Joshua continued. "I need to figure out when…"

Missy lightly touched his arm. "You woke us up at seven," she said.

Yes, but he had wept at his brother's bedside for how long before that?

Martha stood to her feet. "I'll call the hospital," she said.

"And I'll make some coffee," Charles volunteered.

Missy stood as well. "We should call Jamie—and the others."

Charles turned with the coffee filter in his hand. "Is there a way to contact Russell and Garby?"

Joshua's other two brothers—both in prison.

Yes, they would need to be notified as well.

And Bryan's other relatives—his Aunt Yvonne and his niece, Starla.

Things moved quickly after that. It seemed suddenly as if people were everywhere—asking questions—demanding answers.

There wasn't much more that Joshua could tell them.

Platters of food began to arrive even though it was still early in the morning. Someone filled the big coffee machine and another person made tea.

The phone rang constantly. Usually, the person wanted to speak to Joshua but sometimes Missy would answer the questions, accept the condolences…

The doctor came with questions of his own—one's that Joshua did his best to answer. They decided on an approximate time of death.

The doctor signed a death certificate, established that arrangements had already been made for the body, patted Joshua lightly on the arm in farewell, and departed.

Joshua sat down beside the bed, suddenly overcome with grief once more.

It was over. The final goodbye. No more chances. No more time.

"Joshua Quill?"

He turned quickly at the sound of an unfamiliar voice. "Yes…"

The man looked to be only a little older than Joshua himself, but he wore a suit and tie, and his voice and handshake spoke of authority and confidence.

"Robin Finley," he said, by way of introduction.

His manner grew solemn as he looked down at his former client.

But as Joshua had sensed in his phone conversation with Robin, Bryan seemed to have been more than just a client.

"You knew him well?" Joshua asked.

To his surprise, Robin shook his head.

"We met just four months ago—at a mutual friend's Christmas party. We got to talking and…" Robin smiled, remembering. "He asked me if I knew any good lawyers."

Joshua smiled too. That sounded like Bryan all right.

"I think what I remember most about him," Robin continued softly, "was his courage—and of course, his sense of humor."

Robin pulled the desk chair over and sat down adjacent to Joshua. "I'm an estate lawyer," he said, "but I've never been so involved in the time preceding death as I have been with Bryan. He thought of everything. He wanted it to be as easy as possible for Cynarra and for the rest of his family."

His family... Even though they'd had no contact for almost ten years.

"He wanted to have all the details taken care of," Robin continued, "so that there would be time enough to deal with the really important matters in his last hours."

Robin was facing him now, asking the unspoken question: *Had there been enough time?*

"He only arrived here yesterday," Robin prompted.

"Yes," Joshua said.

Robin waited as Joshua collected his thoughts.

How to possibly express all that had happened between them in that short time… And how much did Robin know? How much would there be to explain?

Robin's smile was one of compassion and his voice was kind. "I don't need to know the details," he said. "I don't consider myself a counselor or a priest. But Bryan did specifically want to ask your forgiveness for some things that happened to you as a child. And if he didn't have time, then he requested that I do that on his behalf."

Joshua swallowed back the tears that were threatening to fall again.

"He asked me."

Robin nodded, obviously relieved.

"I forgave him," Joshua continued in an unsteady voice.

"Good." Robin smiled. He looked over to where Bryan's body lay. "I only knew him as a kind and very courageous man—and a loving father."

Joshua felt a twinge of jealousy. He should have been the one to know his brother in that way.

"And you agreed to take Cynarra?" Robin asked, unaware of his thoughts.

"Yes."

Someone knocked on the door. In the stillness of the room, the sound was like a thunderclap. Both Robin and Joshua turned to see who it was.

Michael's head and shoulders appeared. "I'm sorry to interrupt," he said, "but there's a phone call for you, Joshua."

A phone call? There'd been dozens of them this morning. Couldn't someone have taken a message?

Michael stepped into the room, his hand outstretched. "I don't believe we've met…"

Michael hadn't been present earlier in the morning and obviously didn't know about Robin, and Bryan's requests. It was typical of Michael to rush ahead into something without asking questions first.

Robin didn't stand to greet him. He spoke with authority. "Perhaps the phone calls could wait."

Michael raised his eyebrows inquiringly in Joshua's direction.

"This is Robin Finley, Bryan's lawyer," Joshua said in a quietly controlled voice. "We just need a bit more time alone."

Michael whistled. "You called a lawyer already! Must be some pretty big money involved. Gonna get rich again, are you?"

Joshua was too shocked to speak but Robin was on his feet in an instant. "Whoever you are and whatever right you think you have to speak to Mr. Quill in this manner, may I remind you that his brother is very recently deceased and this is a time of bereavement."

"I didn't even think you liked him," Michael challenged Joshua.

But he had been standing in an open doorway and there were others now.

Martha spoke his name sharply and Rosalee tugged at Michael's arm.

Joshua finally found his voice. "We can talk later, Michael."

With a careless shrug, he turned around, shutting the door behind him.

"Who was that?" Robin asked, still obviously shocked by Michael's behavior.

"My wife's cousin." Joshua continued to stare at the closed door.

"He acts like he owns the place."

Joshua sighed. "I think that might be part of the problem."

"He's part owner?" Robin asked.

"No," Joshua said, wondering why he hadn't seen the obvious before, "but I think maybe he thought that he should be."

Robin nodded. "These things can be difficult at times. Bryan, as you might expect, left everything to Cynarra. There is, of course, money available for her living expenses. Bryan was very clear that he didn't want her to be lacking for anything—"

"I don't need his money to do that!" Joshua exclaimed. "She's my brother's daughter. I can take care of her."

"Bryan anticipated that you might feel this way."

Joshua turned away. *Had Bryan anticipated everything?* It made him feel vulnerable and manipulated all over again.

Robin's voice was gentle. "I know this is a lot to take in all at once. And many of these details can wait. But let me just say that if you ever need any money for Cynarra—any unforeseen expenses—there is money available in the estate."

Robin reached into his briefcase and pulled out a thick manila envelope. "I have some things here that you might need right away," he said. "There's Cynarra's birth certificate, health card, immunization card and her school report cards. She seems to have had some excellent tutors…" He handed the envelope to Joshua.

Robin stood to his feet and put out his hand towards Joshua. "I think that's about all for now," he said. "I'll have some other papers ready for you to sign shortly."

Joshua shook his hand as Robin continued, "I'll be in touch."

Joshua stood slowly to his feet. "The—uh—body…" he began.

"They're waiting outside," Robin said in a quiet voice. "I'm assuming that these patio doors open?"

"Yes."

"If you could just unlock them before you leave."

"They're not locked," Joshua said in a voice suddenly choked with emotion. This was it. The wake, the funeral—all condensed into this small little wedge of time.

"Everything will be taken care of," Robin assured him. "The room will be completely cleaned, the bedding removed, and any leftover medications will be disposed of as well. I assume it's all in this room?"

Joshua looked around and walked unsteadily into the bathroom. The purple case was sitting open on top of the toilet tank. *Would*

Cynarra want her case back? He had no answer. *It all seemed to be happening so fast!*

Joshua returned to the bedroom. "I think the medicine is all here—in the bathroom."

"Everything will be taken care of," Robin assured him once more.

Tears sprang suddenly to Joshua's eyes. *Had Bryan planned even these small details? Or did this always happen when a body was donated for research?*

"We can wait a few more minutes. If you need more time…"

Joshua shook his head, lowering his eyes from Robin down to his brother's body.

"I need a whole lifetime." Joshua's voice broke into a deep sob.

Robin walked over, put his arm around him and led him towards the door. "Find comfort in your friends and family," Robin advised.

The people had multiplied since they'd been gone. The loud babble of voices seemed an affront after the quiet of the bedroom.

"If you don't mind," Robin said, "I'll lock this door and go out through the patio doors. We'll unlock it when we're finished."

Joshua shakily agreed. Missy was speaking his name. He heard the door shut and the lock click behind him.

Missy wrapped her arms around him and Joshua buried his face in her shoulder and wept for the brother that he'd never really known.

Chapter 8

Joshua couldn't tear his eyes away from the bedroom door. He could hear some muffled movements from inside…

Missy put a cup of hot coffee in his hands and sat down beside him. Joshua felt Martha's hand on his shoulder. The noise and babble seemed to have receded into the dining area. Joshua was grateful for the little oasis of silence around him.

Suddenly, there was a loud commotion—and Yvonne Quill burst into the kitchen and began shouting at Joshua in Ojibway, a language that he understood but Missy and Martha did not.

Yvonne was angry that no one had called her to her nephew's deathbed. And she was *furious* that she would not be allowed to see him now—or ever. She loudly demanded to know why there would be no wake—or even a funeral.

Her strident voice fell like hammer blows, jarring his already shattered nerves. But he'd never had the strength to stand up against his aunt. She'd always been the stronger of the two, able to reduce him in minutes to feeling like a whipped puppy, cowering from her voice.

She didn't wait for—or necessarily seem to want—any of Joshua's explanations. She didn't allow him room to speak but kept on berating him as he sat with bowed head.

Yvonne accused Joshua of destroying her entire family. She blamed him that both of her other nephews were in jail. And her only niece was dead. And she was no longer allowed to see her grand-niece and grand-nephew…

Joshua slowly lifted his head. His nephew—not allowed to see him?

"He's staying with me for now."

Joshua looked past his aunt to see his niece standing in the doorway. He wondered how long she'd been there. It was certainly a relief to know that Starla was taking care of her little brother.

Yvonne flashed angry eyes towards her grand-niece.

But Starla was being gently led away by her husband, Lewis, and Yvonne directed her wrath upon Joshua once more.

He was especially vulnerable now, exhausted physically and emotionally. He made an easy target…

But there was another voice now. Also speaking in Ojibway. And this one was deeper—and calmer.

Joshua looked up in amazement as Charles gently guided Yvonne away from the kitchen. His words were soothing as he expressed his sympathy for her grief. He offered her a cup of tea and asked if she would like to sit down in one of the comfortable chairs by the fire…

Joshua almost wept with relief.

Suddenly, he heard the lock on the bedroom door click open again.

They were done! They were leaving!

Joshua jumped to his feet and rushed into the bedroom.

A strong breeze blew through the room but the pungent odor of disinfectant still clung in the air. The bed was stripped. The bedside table, empty.

Missy clutched his arm. "Joshua…"

He pulled free and ran towards the patio doors. He yanked the screen door open and ran out onto the deck.

He was just in time to see a large blue van disappear down the road behind some of the buildings. He watched as it reappeared further down the road and then it was gone for good.

He wondered if their plane was fueled and ready to go. And he wondered if he could—or should—follow the van and see the plane off.

Joshua felt Missy's arm slip through his again.

They were alone. No one else had followed his headlong rush into the bedroom. Martha must have shut the door to give them some privacy.

Joshua and Missy sank down onto the top step of the patio.

There were some scattered clouds in the sky—not enough to stop the flight out. A cold wind blew off the lake. Maybe the ice would go out today…

Suddenly, his eyes fastened on the dock. *The dock! Cynarra!*

Joshua jumped to his feet.

"Missy! When did you last see Cynarra?"

"I—I'm not sure." Missy hesitated. "It's been a while…"

But Joshua had heard enough. He ran down the hill towards the lake, scanning the ice even before his feet touched the dock.

It was thin and dark—with no visible breaks in the surface.

Was it possible for the ice to be broken and freeze up again in the short amount of time that she'd been missing?

Joshua glanced at his watch. *It was almost noon!*

He tried to piece together the events of the morning. It must have been about eight o'clock when he'd seen her last—*four hours!*

"Cynarra is up at the lodge."

Joshua spun around at the sound of Charles's voice.

"She told Martha she wanted to be alone. She's up in the nursery, lying down on the bottom bunk where she slept last night. Missy just went up to check on her," he continued calmly.

Joshua felt his heart rate beginning to return to normal but didn't trust his voice to speak yet.

Charles put an arm around his shoulder and guided Joshua back in the direction of the lodge.

Missy was waiting for him at the front door. "Cynarra is upstairs. She just needs some time alone. There's so many people…" Missy gestured around the large front room. Clusters of people were seated around the fire at the south end of the lodge, by the patio at the north end of the lodge, and around tables in between.

Joshua nodded. It was normal for family and friends to gather when there was the death of a loved one. Usually though, there was some natural end to the "wake"—a funeral and a burial. Joshua wondered how long people would stay when there was no formal end to the grieving time.

His thoughts returned to Cynarra. "She's okay?" he asked.

"Not really." Missy sighed. "She's curled up in a little ball with her face to the wall. She wouldn't talk to me—just to tell me that she wanted to be alone. I—I just wish she'd let me comfort her somehow. I just touched her arm a little and she pulled away."

Joshua swallowed past the lump in his throat. For a moment, he couldn't speak then he managed, "She needs time."

Missy nodded. "Yes, you're probably right."

The crowd started to thin out after lunch, people giving parting hugs and assurance of their love and their prayers.

Missy had brought some food up to Cynarra at noon but the little girl had refused to eat and had remained turned away from her the whole time that Missy was in the room.

Martha had agreed with Joshua. "Give her some time—and space," she advised.

By two o'clock, only Martha and Charles remained, visiting with Missy and Joshua in the kitchen.

"You look tired, honey," Martha said to Missy. "Why don't you go upstairs and lie down for a while?"

"That's a good idea," Joshua agreed.

Charles raised an eyebrow in his direction. "And you look like you're about ready to fall over."

Joshua smiled wanly. He did feel weary to the bone. But although most of the people had left, there were still frequent phone calls, which Joshua felt he should answer in person.

"You get any sleep at all last night?" Charles persisted.

Joshua shook his head.

"It might do you both a world of good…" Martha advised.

But then there was a phone call—and another—and, in the end, only Missy went up to their room to rest.

She was back just a few minutes later. Her face was flushed and she was out of breath. "Cynarra's not in her room!"

Joshua quickly ended his phone call. "Maybe in the bathroom…" he suggested.

Missy shook her head. "I looked in all of the upstairs rooms, just in case."

Martha and Charles stood to their feet. "We'll help you look for her," Charles said.

The four of them searched every possible spot she could be inside the lodge.

"Her backpack is gone," Missy said, after making another thorough search of all the upstairs rooms.

Joshua grabbed a jacket and headed for the door. Charles called out, "Wait! I'll call some people and we'll do an organized search."

Joshua didn't break stride as he said over his shoulder, "I'll be starting to look in the meantime."

He headed straight for the lake again, anxiously scanning the shoreline. It was the most dangerous spot this time of the year. The ice was so thin that it wouldn't even support the weight of a small child.

It was a matter of minutes before Joshua heard the sounds of vehicles returning and then people calling out Cynarra's name as they searched around the property.

The chief of police, Colin Hill, arrived with his deputy, Keegan Littledeer, their squad car lights flashing. It was Colin who rallied everyone back inside the lodge to begin a more organized search.

Joshua reluctantly went back in as well.

"We've put an announcement on the community radio," Charles said. "People will be on the lookout for her."

"She can't have gone far," Missy said in a fretful voice.

"Where have you checked so far?" Colin asked.

A jumble of voices replied and Colin held up his hand for silence. He turned to Keegan. "It'd be good if we had a map of the area."

"I've got something we can use," Joshua interjected. He walked quickly to the desk at the north end of the lodge. There was a detailed map of the entire property there—a blueprint drawn up by a surveyor when the property was transferred over to Joshua. It showed all the rooms of the lodge and each of the cabins as well as all of the other buildings that remained on the former mine property.

He stretched the large sheet out on one of the tables and weighted the corners down.

With a thick black marker, Colin began to X out each spot that had been already searched.

His task was hampered by Joshua who asked each person if they were sure—if they had checked every small nook and cranny. "She's small and she's smart," he said.

"But honey…" Missy protested when he questioned her, "do you really think that Cynarra would purposely hide from us?"

Joshua sighed. "I don't know. She may just want to be alone. And that's fine. But if she's lost or hurt, I—" His voice broke.

What would he do if something happened to the little girl?

He'd promised Bryan!

"We'll find her," Missy whispered.

Joshua nodded briefly in her direction before turning his attention back to Colin and the people who were reporting in. It seemed the entire property had been given a thorough search.

There was no tall grass this time of year—and there was no deep snow either. The trees were bare, making for better visibility in the bush as well.

"We need to call in the Crisis Response Team," Colin finally said. Joshua quickly agreed. If Cynarra was lost or hurt…

Joshua made the phone call himself. He took Cynarra's birth certificate out of the manila envelope that Robin had given him… She was going to be eight years old in less than a month. He described what she was wearing when they'd last seen her—including the dark green packsack, which she had probably taken with her.

As he answered their questions, he frequently consulted with Missy. They decided that she was around four feet tall but they couldn't get it more precise than that. She was very slightly built but Joshua didn't want to try to guess what her weight might be—he really had no idea.

And he couldn't help but wonder what difference it would make anyway. There couldn't possibly be two little girls wandering around lost in the bush, could there? It wasn't as if they were going to zoom in for a close look, decide she wasn't the right height and leave her there to die!

Joshua didn't say what he was thinking. But he was getting edgier and more impatient as the moments passed.

Now they wanted to know how long she'd been missing.

Too long!

"I don't know," Joshua growled into the receiver, "Maybe an hour or two or three…" He looked at his watch. It was five minutes past three o'clock.

"You don't know how long she's been missing?" the voice queried.

"Just find her!" Joshua yelled.

He felt the phone being eased out of his hands. Colin spoke in soothing tones. "Let me talk to them, okay?"

Joshua strode away from the phone.

"I'm going out to look for her," he announced.

Charles called out, "Wait!" and Joshua walked reluctantly back towards the older man. "I need to go find her," Joshua said.

Colin was off the phone and his voice carried the authority of his position as police chief. He spoke to Joshua but his voice was loud enough to reach everyone else in the large dining area. "We have a Crisis Response Team on their way. They should be here in an hour or so. We will wait for them and coordinate our efforts with them. You…" he said, motioning towards Joshua. "You can make a list of any possible places she might have gone. Maybe to her cousin's house or Yvonne's."

"Or maybe over to see the twins…" Martha suggested.

Joshua shook his head angrily. She wouldn't go to the houses of people she had barely met.

"I'll start making a list," Missy said. She looked around the room, full again with friends and family. "But I think word has gotten around that she's missing…"

Joshua knew he had to go look for her. He would go crazy just waiting around, doing nothing.

He walked through the kitchen, into the guest bedroom and out the patio doors. Once outside, though, he paused, unsure of where to go. The entire mine property had been searched—but how thoroughly?

Goldrock Lodge had been built against a rock face that rose high above it. From the downstairs patio, where Joshua stood, a set of steps began that led up to the second story balcony and then on up to the top of the rock where a gazebo-like structure stood. It wasn't the highest observation point around—the old mine headframe was—but it was high enough to observe at least a ten mile circumference around the Goldrock Lodge property.

Joshua thought he might get a better idea of where Cynarra might have gone if he could get a bird's eye view of the area.

He walked to the top and looked all around. From where he stood, he could look north to where Rabbit Lake spilled into Pine River. There was an old road that headed off that way, winding its way along the shore until it reached the old Robertson's Mine— a long-abandoned open-pit mine that was great for motorcycling or four-wheeling. To the south, the community of Rabbit Lake stretched out along the shore of the lake for which it was named. Joshua shaded his eyes and looked out over Macaroni Bay, a nice quiet spot to paddle a canoe or learn to swim. The waves on Rabbit Lake could get pretty high when a storm blew in. Now, the entire bay was covered in thin, dark ice, a bit darker in a line that headed south, marking where the winter ice road had been.

Behind him, Joshua knew there was the remnants of the old road that had gone all the way south 150 miles to the highway on which a person could travel another 100 or so miles to meet the TransCanada highway that transversed the country east to west. Though it sounded quite accessible, Rabbit Lake was actually fairly remote, especially at this time of the year. People could take the ice road in the winter and boat out during the summer but in the springtime, most people had to fly out of the community if they wanted to travel.

The old road south had been in use for a few years when the gold mine was in operation but after a large portion of it was flooded out, most of the road was allowed to fall into disrepair. Parts of it, closer to the community, were kept open by hunters and trappers. Joshua was unable to see it from where he stood but knew that he could access it from the north end of the lodge.

As Joshua looked around and thought about where Cynarra might have gone, he kept coming back to the idea that she would want to go home—back to what she had known as her home—in Toronto.

She and Bryan would have flown from Toronto to Winnipeg so Cynarra would know that she first had to get to Winnipeg. Would she try to stowaway on a plane? Or perhaps she had enough money to buy a ticket! But surely someone would have mentioned seeing her at the airport. There had been a community announcement on the radio—people would be looking out for her.

Joshua shook his head. He was thinking too logically and practically. Cynarra was only seven years old and in the depths of grief. She wouldn't necessarily be thinking logically or practically.

She might just want to go somewhere to be alone—or she might think she could somehow walk her way out. A seven year old wouldn't necessarily have a good idea of time and distance.

Joshua squinted into the sun hanging in the sky and wondered if she would know which way was south. She did seem pretty smart—and Robin had mentioned that Bryan seemed to have hired very good tutors for her.

Growing restless again, Joshua knew he had to go and look for her. He just couldn't wait and do nothing until the Crisis Response Team showed up.

Suddenly decisive, Joshua headed down the steps and through the side entrance, and down the narrow passage into the kitchen. He knew he had to find Missy first—she would worry if he was gone for any length of time.

She was sitting at the kitchen table, sipping some herbal tea, and Joshua could see by the brief flash of relief in her eyes that he had been right to let her know he was going.

Unfortunately, Michael and Rosalee were also in the kitchen, Rosalee sitting with Missy, and Michael lounging up against the counter. Joshua looked at Missy as he said in a quiet voice, "I'm going out to look for her."

"We were told to wait," Michael declared.

"They should be here soon," Rosalee added.

Missy stood to her feet. "I'll get a packsack for you."

Joshua smiled gratefully at her and watched as she went back into the passageway from where he'd come and got a packsack and jacket that were hanging there. She filled the packsack with two bottles of water and two wrapped sandwiches and an apple. "Do you think you'll need a flashlight?" she asked.

"What's this?" Michael exclaimed. "You're going off on some major expedition or what?"

"The sun will be setting in just a couple of hours," Missy said, a defensive edge to her voice.

"In three and one half hours," Michael argued, pointing to the kitchen clock.

Missy ignored him. "Do you have your pocket-knife?"

Joshua patted the pouch on his belt. "As always," he said.

"Do you have a lighter?"

"How about a tent and sleeping bag?" Michael quipped.

Rosalee hit him playfully in the arm. "Shh!" she said as they exchanged grins.

"I'll be praying for you," Missy said softly.

"And for Cynarra," he requested.

Missy wrapped her arms around him and Joshua hugged her in return. "I love you," she whispered.

"Love you, too," he said.

There was a dramatic sigh from Michael. "Guess I'd better go with you."

"You don't have to," Joshua quickly responded.

"I'll go," Michael said in a resigned tone.

Rosalee put two sandwiches in a bag for him.

Michael said, "No need for that. We'll be back before supper."

"We'll probably be having sandwiches for supper, so you might as well take some," Rosalee said wryly, surveying the platters of food that had multiplied since word got out that there was a search party planned.

Michael took a can of Pepsi out of the refrigerator, tossed it into the packsack along with the extra sandwiches and asked cheerily, "Now, how are we going to sneak out past the police?"

"Go out through the garage," Missy said, her tone still serious. "I'll tell Colin later."

"So, where we goin'?" Michael asked when they were outside of the lodge.

"The old mine road," Joshua said, gesturing to where the road angled up and around the rock outcropping before heading south.

Michael hit him on the arm. "Okay, buddy, let's hit the trail."

Even as the road grew steeper, Michael kept up the carefree banter.

When it flattened out, Joshua began jogging but after a few minutes of Michael's loud complaints, slowed to a fast walk.

"This ain't a race," Michael quipped. "Don't know what your hurry is."

Joshua was in no mood to talk and certainly no mood to argue.

But Michael was able to keep up a conversation single-handedly.

Joshua wished he could tune him out. But Michael had known him too long—and he knew which buttons to push.

But why? That's what Joshua couldn't figure out.

After almost an hour of putting up with it, Joshua finally spun around and demanded. *"Why are you doing this?"*

Michael looked startled—but only for an instant. Then his face broke into a friendly grin. "Just helping you out, man."

"Helping *me*?"

"Yeah, you look like somethin' the cat drug in," Michael quipped. "I'm here to help you when you finally trip over your own feet. Maybe I'll sling you over my back and carry ya home or somethin'."

Joshua stared at him. Then he shook his head and kept walking.

"If you're so concerned about me, then why are you trying so hard to make me angry?"

"I don't have to do anything to make *you* angry," Michael retorted. "You're like an emotional time bomb—always ready to explode at the slightest little thing."

"That's not true," Joshua said without breaking stride.

"Like take right now, for instance," Michael insisted. "Instead of going about this with a clear head, you're running off like some bull in a china shop!"

No, Tom had been the wild bull. Joshua was the lone stallion.

"You don't want to work with the rest of the community. You insist on going your own way. I don't know what my grandfather ever saw in you!"

Now they were getting to the heart of the matter…

But Michael was strangely silent after that.

He kept a couple of paces behind Joshua but he didn't speak again for almost an hour—an amazing feat for Michael!

Joshua appreciated the silence but he worried about their relationship. Michael and Rosalee were not only friends; they were valued co-workers. Was it all about to end?

"I need to take a break," Michael announced suddenly.

Joshua stopped to look back. Michael had found a fallen log near a large pine tree, and leaning back up against the tree trunk, he gave a huge sigh. "You gotta remember," he said, "I grew up in the city. I haven't been traipsing through the bush all my life. And I don't know why you people call this a road…"

"We don't call it a road," Joshua spoke evenly. "And if you're tired, I'll just go on ahead."

Michael sighed even louder and rose slowly and deliberately. "No, I've sworn allegiance to my king." He put his right hand over his heart as he spoke the words with a false accent and the feigned resignation of a martyr.

Joshua shook his head angrily. "Nobody asked you to come along."

The drone of a plane interrupted their conversation. They both looked up as it passed overhead.

"They're probably thinking—*what a bunch of idiots!*" Michael mused.

"Because we're doing a foot search—and they're doing an aerial one?"

"No." Michael rolled his eyes. "Because we're obviously searching in the wrong place."

"Why do you say that?" Joshua demanded. "Did you see her somewhere else today? Why didn't you mention something earlier?"

Michael shook his head in disgust. "No, I didn't see her at all today. But there is no way in the world that any city kid in their right mind would go to all the trouble of taking this *road*. It doesn't even lead anywhere anymore, does it?"

"No," Joshua said, "But Cynarra wouldn't know that. And somebody was down this way with an ATV not too long ago. You can see the tracks. This old road looks like it could lead somewhere. It once did."

"Yeah, whatever…" Michael spoke dismissively.

Joshua started walking again.

And Michael followed reluctantly behind.

Chapter 9

"OKAY, TIME TO HEAD BACK," Michael declared.

Joshua turned to stare at him.

"We've been walking for two hours," Michael explained. "If we walk two hours back, we still won't get there before dark. It's time to head back."

"I have a flashlight," Joshua said, trying to keep the annoyance out of his voice.

"Well, I don't," Michael said. "What I do have is a brain—something that you obviously parked about ten miles back."

"Six," Joshua corrected. "If it's been two hours, we've likely gone about six miles."

"Six—ten—what does it matter? How far you plannin' to go anyway?"

Joshua sighed. "Until I find her."

Michael rolled his eyes. "And what if you don't? You planning to walk all night?"

"The road is flooded over about twenty miles in. If I haven't found her by then, I'll head back."

Michael stared at him incredulously. "You're kidding, right?"

Joshua sighed again. "No Michael, I'm not kidding."

"Man, you is crazy!"

Crazy or desperate… Whatever he was, Joshua knew he needed to keep going. If Cynarra had gone down this road, she could have had as much as a three or four hour start on them.

And Joshua especially didn't want her to be alone out here at night. Even if he was on a wild goose chase, he'd take a chance on that. He'd spent many nights alone in the bush; he wasn't afraid to spend another. But it was an entirely different matter with Cynarra. As far as Joshua knew, she'd never even been out camping before.

Michael of course, argued long and hard.

Joshua kept walking, forcing Michael to follow him if he persisted in keeping up with the argument.

Joshua just wished he would leave—turn around and go back alone.

But it wasn't to be that easy.

Michael was just as determined to make Joshua give up, as Joshua was to keep going. It was a battle of wills between two very strong-willed young men.

"You just want to be a hero!" Michael accused.

"No, I want Cynarra to be found and I don't care who finds her."

"Maybe she's found already. Did you ever think of that?"

Joshua patted the cell phone case looped on his belt. "They would have called us," he said.

"We're probably out of range," Michael said, pulling out his cell. "Yep—no service."

Joshua shrugged. He was going to keep on. If they'd found her, that was wonderful—but if they hadn't…

"So what am I supposed to tell them when I arrive back alone?" Michael demanded.

Joshua sighed. "Tell them anything you like."

"And when you still haven't returned tomorrow?"

Joshua kept walking.

"Then they'll probably want to send out a search party for you!" Michael continued. "And then everybody will be worried about poor little Joshua."

Joshua spun around. "Why do you care?"

"Because it's always about you! Always!"

Joshua shook his head. "No, this is about Cynarra."

"No!" Michael yelled. "It's always been about you! Always! Grandpa and I used to play chess together all the time—before you showed up! We used to talk together—about our dreams and plans. We used to talk about what *I* would do when *I* grew up. Then you came along. Then it was Joshua this and Joshua that!"

Michael's face was inches away from his now. Joshua stood his ground as Michael delivered his final verbal assault. "He would have left the camp to me—if you hadn't come along!"

Joshua nodded slowly. "You could be right, Michael."

Suddenly, he felt tired. Too tired to go on and even too tired to think about the long walk back.

He slipped his backpack off and slumped down in front of a tree, leaning his back wearily against the solid trunk.

"*Now* you want to rest!" Michael spoke tersely.

"Just for a while."

"And then what?" Michael demanded.

Joshua shook his head wearily. "I don't know. Maybe I'll go on; maybe I'll go back."

Michael waved his hand in disgust. "Whatever!"

"Michael…"

He had turned to walk back towards the camp. Michael stopped, but didn't look back.

"I'm sorry that I came between your grandpa and you. I never meant for that to happen."

Michael paused an instant longer but still didn't turn back to speak or even to look at Joshua.

Fatigue swept over him like a tidal wave.

It would be so easy just to go to sleep.

And maybe Cynarra *had* already been found…

No. No, he had to keep on.

Joshua lifted his packsack, felt its weight and remembered the sandwiches and water that Missy had packed.

He drank one whole bottle of water with barely a breath in between.

I must have been thirsty, he thought. And getting himself dehydrated wouldn't help Cynarra. If he had to carry her back…

Joshua opened one of the packs of sandwiches and began eating.

He'd been hungry too!

Joshua felt remarkably better when he began walking again. The short rest and food had made more of a difference than he thought it would.

Evening shadows were beginning to fall and Joshua was glad that there wasn't any leaf cover. And the sky had completely cleared as well. He tried to remember if the moon would be out or not. His ancestors would have known, walking this trail without the use of watches or calendars…

It was good to be alone, out in the bush.

It was giving him time to think… about Bryan… and his other brothers… and his sister Rebecca… and Cynarra… and Missy… and their new baby… and the youth program.

It was what he needed to do—get away into the bush and just have time to sort things out a bit.

He'd spent way too much time inside this past winter—working on the youth program, trying to keep the books straight, trying to run the camp, trying to coordinate everything alone.

A lone stallion...

Well, he'd let people help him more now.

If Charles could help him with some of the business end of things... And Martha seemed willing to help too. Joshua had thought it would be too painful for her to be back at the lodge with Tom gone. But maybe it would even help her in some way—to be a part of fulfilling Tom's dream.

He sure didn't know what to do about Michael.

And if Michael left, then Rosalee would too.

And maybe Keegan was dissatisfied also.

The program had been just a trial run. He had asked them to give him feedback on what needed to be changed.

They had to decide what direction to take next.

Maybe he should just forget about everything.

Raise a family—live his life. He had Cynarra to think of now, too. She would need a lot of care.

Cynarra... *He had to find her!*

Maybe he should just head back—be part of a regular search party.

But by the time he got back, they would have stopped the search for the night. Everyone would be advised to go home and get some rest—and start fresh in the morning. But Joshua knew there would be no rest for him if Cynarra hadn't been found yet—if she was lost in the bush somewhere—possibly even injured...

But Michael could be right. Cynarra might have gone in a totally different direction. There might be some part of one of the old mine buildings that they hadn't searched thoroughly enough...

Maybe she'd even been found already.

But he just couldn't bear the thought of her being out in the bush alone—especially at this time of the year.

No, he'd keep going—until he found her.

BY THE TIME MICHAEL RETURNED alone, Missy was almost at the end of her rope. She was tired and worried. And she was angry now, too.

She was angry at Joshua for continuing on alone. But she was even angrier at her cousin, Michael, for *allowing* Joshua to go on alone.

"His brother just died! He hasn't slept since the night before last. His niece is lost in the bush somewhere. Couldn't you have at least stayed with him—or talked him into coming back?"

They were sitting around a lit fire in the big stone fireplace, Michael ensconced in the chair that had been Grandpa Tom's favorite, Rosalee hovering over him with a cup of coffee and a plate of sandwiches.

He looked tired. And, for Michael, strangely quiet.

Rosalee came quickly to his defense. "Michael just got done hiking through the bush for over four hours. Maybe you should cut him a bit of slack, Missy. Joshua shouldn't have gone out there in the first place. At least Michael went with him. It's not his fault he couldn't talk him into coming back."

Michael hadn't touched the coffee or sandwiches. He rose slowly to his feet and took his wife's arm. "Let's go. I'm tired."

He stopped for a moment in front of Missy. His eyes narrowed and his voice cut with the venom of sarcasm, "Maybe, you shouldn't have married a *lone stallion*."

She watched them walk away.

A man from the Crisis Response Team was directing people to go home for the night. Friends and family were being strongly advised to wait until morning to resume the organized ground search.

As each person took their leave, Missy felt more and more alone.

If only Joshua were here…

Missy covered her mouth, trying to hold back a sob and raced for the bathroom where she could be alone.

But she hadn't counted on her grandma's keen eye. Martha knocked on the door, waited a moment and then walked in to find Missy leaning against the sink, still trying to hold it all in.

With Martha's warm embrace, the floodgates opened and Martha continued to hold Missy close as she cried all her tears.

"It's okay, honey," Martha said gently. "It's okay. The Lord's watching over the both of them."

"You should sleep now," she advised after helping Missy wash her face. "There isn't anything more that any of us can do tonight. Joshua will be fine. He knows the bush. Maybe this time alone will even be good for him. I know he's got a lot of things to think about."

"I don't think I can sleep," Missy protested. "I'll wait up for Joshua. He should be back soon."

"Joshua would want you to get some sleep," Martha gently chided. "And you gotta take care of my new little great-grandbaby…"

Missy finally allowed herself to be persuaded to have a cup of hot chocolate and go to bed. Martha promised to be close by if Missy needed her.

But as she had predicted, Missy found it impossible to sleep. She finally got out of bed and got dressed again. She wrapped herself in a blanket and sat by the north patio doors, where the old mine road wound past before joining with the front drive.

When Joshua returned, she would see him.

Missy left the patio light on. It lit part of the path before the darkness swallowed it up.

Missy prayed and dozed a little, woke and prayed some more…

THE MOON HAD APPEARED FULL and bright. Joshua's path was lit up almost as if it were day. He turned off his flashlight, glad to save on the batteries. He'd cut down a young poplar and stripped off its bark to make himself a walking stick. It helped him to keep his balance over the rough spots, made more difficult by the crippling fatigue that was dragging at his heels.

He still hadn't seen any sign at all that Cynarra had gone this way. The ground was still hard and frozen, and patches of snow remained in the shadier spots. But she would have gone around the snow, if possible choosing the drier ground to walk on.

He wondered how long it would be before she gave up and started walking back—or if she would.

And he wondered why it was that he was becoming increasingly sure that she had taken this trail.

He had found no evidence to either confirm or deny his suspicions.

Was it possible that the Lord was leading him?

Joshua realized with a start that he hadn't prayed at all since beginning his search. Missy had said that she would pray. And he knew that others would be. Martha and Charles, Jamie and Colin and Sarah…

But Joshua knew that he needed to pray, too.

"Oh God," he whispered, "I need you now. If I'm way off base here, please let me know. But if Cynarra did take this path, it would be good—it would be *really good* if I could just have some kind of a sign. And please Lord, wherever she is, take care of her. She's gone through so much in the last two days. If she's hurt or in some kind of danger..."

As he prayed, he began to walk faster.

Some of the fallen trees could be easily stepped over and some of them walked under. But he had to climb over some of them and this slowed him down.

He didn't want to be slowed down—not now.

It was as if every minute counted—no, every second!

He ran on the smoother parts.

The urgency grew within him with every passing moment.

The thought flashed in his mind that maybe he was just overtired, overstressed... There'd been a lot happening recently...

Maybe he was going crazy.

It had to be sheer madness to be racing through the bush at this hour of the night at this time of the year. Even with the moonlight, smaller rocks and branches were not always visible and Joshua almost fell a couple of times as he tripped over unseen obstacles, his walking stick saving him in the last instant.

He finally had to stop for a rest but wouldn't allow himself the luxury of sitting. He only leaned against a tree for a few minutes. If he sat down, he might sleep. And if he slept, he might not be in time.

In time for what?

There were no answers. Just the overwhelming need to hurry... hurry...

Joshua began running again.

He had to hurry.

Run fast… *Run faster!*

He couldn't think about being tired. He couldn't think about sore muscles and joints.

He had to be on time!

He had to be!

IT COULD HAVE BEEN A RABBIT—caught by a lynx or a bobcat.

Their death cry sounded exactly like a human scream. He'd heard it many times before.

But Joshua knew it wasn't a rabbit this time.

It was Cynarra!

He pushed himself even harder than before. She was just up ahead…

He saw the wild animal before he saw her. The black bear was skinny from a long winter's hibernation but it looked big stretched out to its full length as it reached up to claw at the little girl with the large backpack, who was frantically trying to find a higher branch to grab hold of.

"Nooo!" Joshua cried out as the claws dug deep into Cynarra's right leg.

The bear, startled by his cry, turned to face him.

Joshua raised his walking stick and began yelling. "Get out of here! Go on! Get!"

The bear came down on all fours but still didn't seem inclined to leave.

When it glanced back at Cynarra, still clinging to the tree, Joshua swung his stick like a baseball bat, hitting the bear's tender snout as it turned to look back at him.

With a loud bawling sound, the bear turned and lumbered off into the bush.

Joshua dropped his stick and grabbed Cynarra as she climbed down within his reach. She clung tightly to him as he began to run back the way he had come.

He slowed his pace when he shifted her in his arms and felt the warm blood from her leg wound on his hand. He needed to stop and look at the wound.

She was trembling and sobbing. She needed his reassurance, too.

Joshua tried to gently set Cynarra down on the ground but she fought him, frantically clawing at his neck and shoulders, wanting to be held again, wanting to continue to run away. She was crying and mumbling incoherently but Joshua understood.

"We're safe now, Cynarra. The bear is far, far away. You're safe now."

"Run... please... run..." she begged.

"No," he said gently, "you're safe now, Cynarra. Black bears don't usually attack people—especially not big people like me. And I hit him hard right on the nose—he won't be back."

"He—he might..." Cynarra said between deep shuddering breaths as her sobbing subsided.

He was on his knees now with her still clinging tightly to his neck.

"I'll stand in front of you if he comes back," Joshua promised. "I'll protect you—with my life."

Her fierce grip relaxed a little. "You—you will?"

"Yes," Joshua said softly, greatly relieved that his words had calmed her. "I will stand in front of you and protect you."

Her eyes grew wide. "With your life?" she asked in a voice filled with awe.

Joshua smiled. "With my life," he vowed.

"Now, I need to take a look at your leg," he said, gently easing off her packsack and lowering her the rest of the way to the ground.

Joshua gasped as he saw that the claws had torn her flesh right to the bone, leaving a five inch long gaping wound on the back of her calf.

"It doesn't hurt," Cynarra said bravely.

It will…

And the wound was bleeding profusely, exacerbated by the jostling while he ran. Joshua knew he needed to get a pressure bandage on it immediately.

He quickly peeled off his jacket and sweatshirt. He had only a light T-shirt underneath and the air felt cold on his arms.

Cynarra was trembling. From the cold or perhaps from shock… Joshua didn't know. He put his jacket around her as a blanket; his sweatshirt would provide soft bandages.

Joshua got out his pocketknife and quickly cut it into strips.

Cynarra began to cry as he wound the bandages tightly around the wound. And Joshua realized in that instant that he would have done anything—anything—to take her pain away. Gladly he would have taken her place if he could have.

He prayed silently as he worked—prayed earnestly for a miracle.

They were at least six hours away from medical treatment—*if* he could keep up the pace that he had on the way in…

He had to try. She was at risk for infection and, although he'd tried to bind up the wound as best he could, Cynarra had still lost a lot of blood.

He took a quick look through her backpack and found it still contained half a dozen ham sandwiches, likely what had attracted the bear to Cynarra. It saddened him to see all those sandwiches—how far has she intended to walk?

He gave Cynarra as much water as she would drink and then finished off the bottle, wishing he had brought more along. She didn't want any of the sandwiches but Joshua ate one, knowing he would need his strength for the walk back. He rolled up his packsack and put it inside hers. He put the packsack on, wrapped Cynarra in his coat and lifted her up again.

Tears were rolling down her cheeks but she wasn't making a sound.

So brave…

He began to talk to her as he walked. He kept his voice quiet and calm, hoping that it would soothe her—or at least distract her from the pain.

"You had us pretty worried when we found out you were missing," he said. "We looked all around the lodge and all the other buildings, too…"

Joshua was thankful he hadn't spent any more time looking through the buildings or around the property. He wondered if the Crisis Response Team had ordered another search and he wondered how far they'd gotten before calling it quits for the night. He knew the usual plan was to work out in concentric circles going further and further away from where the person had last been seen.

Would they have started down any of the roads or trails and if so, which ones…

Joshua's thoughts began to run together and he realized that fatigue was starting to catch up with him again. How many hours had he been without sleep now? He tried to calculate but the numbers swam in his head.

"Tell me about…"

Joshua bent closer to hear Cynarra's faint voice.

"...Growing up with my father."

That shocked him awake!

His first instinct was to deny her request.

But she was being so brave. And he needed *something* to concentrate his thoughts on.

But there was nothing good, nothing happy about the years that he and Bryan had spent together. And there had been a big age difference...

"Summers were warm..." he began, speaking slowly and trying to think fast as he felt his way forward. "We had a canoe, a beautiful cedar strip, that cut through the water like a Viking ship when we paddled her hard. And she floated gentle as a leaf when we let her drift."

Joshua glanced down. Cynarra's eyes were closed but there was just the faintest of smiles. And Joshua knew then that he would keep telling her stories all night... if it would help in some small way.

Cynarra opened her eyes. "Were there any birds?" she asked.

"Tons!" Joshua smiled.

And Cynarra closed her eyes again and smiled too.

"There were beautiful swans..."

Cynarra's eyes flashed open.

Joshua chuckled. "Okay, so there weren't any swans. There were loons. They're not as beautiful. They're actually kinda ugly. They have these little red beady eyes. But they're very graceful and they're excellent swimmers. You can be paddling along and they'll suddenly dip under the water and then just as suddenly, they'll reappear a long ways away from where they dove. You never really know where they'll pop up again. And they have this really awesome call that they make to one another. I could do a loon call for you—uh—if I had my hands free..."

Joshua talked on and on, mile after mile. Bryan's name was never mentioned but Joshua told Cynarra about all the things he loved... the water... the bush... But most of the stories he told were not from his childhood but from the years after Tom Peters had taken him in. That's when they'd built the beautiful cedar strip that he still loved to paddle on a quiet summer evening.

He told Cynarra all about the different birds and animals in the area, the berries that could be picked in the summer, how good they tasted in pie...

She might have occasionally drifted off but Joshua knew it was his voice that was having a calming effect on her—and distracting her from the pain. As soon as he stopped talking, she would begin to stir again.

As the hours passed, Joshua found it increasingly difficult to keep his thoughts focused. He shifted from topic to topic, knowing he was rambling, knowing that Cynarra didn't really care as long as he kept talking.

And walking.

That's all he had to do. Keep talking—and keep walking. But Joshua was feeling clumsier by the minute. It was becoming increasingly difficult for him to not stumble over rocks and fallen branches. Even a slight dip in the path threw off his balance.

He desperately tried not to jar Cynarra, knowing that every time he stumbled a little, it caused her pain. Unprepared for the sudden movement, her first response was a quick intake of breath and a low moan. But as Joshua quickly apologized and righted himself again, the little girl quieted immediately. He could still feel the tension in her body as she tried to maintain control—tried not to cry or complain in any way.

She was a tough little kid. Though he most desperately wished for her sake, that the path could be smoother, easier…

But her path through life hadn't been smooth or easy either.

And Joshua knew that he wanted with all his heart to change that—to give her a secure home and a loving extended family.

Bryan, to be fair, had done his best. She had grown up feeling loved—a priceless and essential gift for any child.

But she was far too serious and responsible for her age. He knew what it was like to grow up like that. And Joshua wanted more than that for Cynarra. He wanted her to have fun—to play games—to laugh with friends.

Joshua imagined her at their Christmas community celebrations. There would be games and relays, tons of food and music, gifts for the children and an enormously fun hockey tournament where the teams all dressed up in costumes trying each year to outdo one another.

Joshua spoke what was on his mind, describing in detail the festivities of the year before.

And he talked about things they could do in the summer, too.

They could go out on the lake and go fishing and camping. He'd make sure that she learned how to swim. And he'd teach her how to run a boat motor and how to paddle a canoe and how to set up a tent and how to cook fish and bannock over an open fire…

Joshua's voice grew hoarse as he continued to talk and walk mile after mile.

Most of the time, Cynarra was limp and still in his arms. He was tempted sometimes to ask for a response but her voice was so faint that he had to stop and listen for her answer. And every time he stopped, it took a tremendous effort to start walking again. Joshua knew he dared not stop and rest. That would be the end for sure.

As he stumbled on mile after mile, his voice grew hoarser and it was an effort to keep his thoughts untangled enough to mumble anything coherent. His arms trembled with the strain of carrying his small burden and pain shot through his back and neck. His legs, long heavy with fatigue, now sometimes felt as if they weren't even there anymore. Joshua had to fight against a weird floating sensation that was perhaps his worst enemy. Sounds of the forest were amplified, startling his shattered nerves. The path wavered like a mirage as moonbeams skittered through the bare tree branches.

Each step forward required a tremendous effort of his will.

But he had to keep going for Cynarra's sake. For Cynarra…

Chapter 10

Missy had stayed by the window through the long hours of the night.

She sat huddled in her blanket, feeling chilled to the bone but turning up the central heat didn't seem to help a lot. She knew that the trembling feeling, inside and outside of her body, was not from the cold but from fear.

She'd been praying almost non-stop and even when not actually speaking the words, her heart was crying out to her Heavenly Father—and she knew He heard every sigh and saw every tear.

But rather than the peace that He so often granted her in difficult moments, Missy instead felt as if she needed to keep on praying—as if she was engaged in a life and death battle.

She mostly sat curled up in the corner of the couch facing the window. But occasionally she walked around a little. Once or twice, she actually walked out onto the patio and was tempted to continue down the trail—just a little ways, she told herself. But common sense fortunately overruled.

She'd glanced frequently at the clock throughout the night, watching the slow progression of minutes into hours.

It was almost five o'clock. Soon the day would begin again. And the search parties would be sent out…

Missy pulled the blanket up around her shoulders and turned her eyes back to the window.

Someone was out there!

Coming down the path...

Staggering as if he were drunk...

Carrying a small child...

Missy threw aside the blanket and ran to open the patio door.

Joshua... *Joshua!*

He didn't see her!

He was mumbling something about Christmas!

"Joshua..."

Suddenly, his eyes lit with recognition.

But he was swaying like grass in the wind.

Missy rushed forward and took Cynarra from his arms.

He smiled at her—so glad—so glad—to be home.

Then with a soft sigh, he fell backwards onto the hard concrete patio.

"Grandma!" Missy screamed, kneeling down beside her husband with Cynarra still in her arms. "Grandma!" she screamed louder. "Help! Help me!"

Cynarra stirred in her arms and opened her eyes. Missy saw pain and fear there, and she controlled her voice, not letting the panic she felt overcome her. "It's okay. You're okay now," she said gently.

Martha called to her and Missy yelled, "Out here!"

She heard Martha gasp and felt her own heart constrict as her grandmother knelt down and reached for Joshua's pulse.

"Set her down and go call an ambulance," Martha commanded.

Missy quickly obeyed, running back into the lodge and grabbing the cordless phone from beside the couch.

She turned back and almost collapsed with fear and grief.

Martha was giving Joshua CPR!

With trembling fingers, Missy dialed the number for the Emergency Medical Services.

Her call was answered on the first ring. Missy forced herself to speak clearly. "This is Missy Quill—at Goldrock Lodge. We need help—medical help…"

"Okay, Dan here. Can you tell me who is hurt and—?"

Missy's firm resolve shattered. "We need help now!" she screamed.

"We're on our way to the camp," Dan said. "Don't hang up. I'll talk to you as we go."

"No! Just drive fast. Don't talk."

"My partner's driving fast," Dan replied calmly. "Now, can you tell me who is hurt? There might be something you can do to help."

"Grandma's giving him CPR—Joshua—Joshua, my husband." Missy fell on her knees beside them. He still wasn't moving. She couldn't tell if he was breathing or not.

A low moan came from Cynarra, and Missy tore her eyes away from her husband. The bandages on Cynarra's leg were soaked scarlet with blood. "There's a little girl too," she said breathlessly into the phone. "She's hurt."

And then she heard them, crunching over the loose stones, sending them flying up under the vehicle, pummeling the undercarriage like pellets of hail.

Four Emergency Medical Technicians spilled out of the vehicle and Missy and Martha were both asked to step aside as people and equipment suddenly filled the small area around Joshua and Cynarra.

Missy turned tear-filled eyes towards Martha. "What happened to them, Grandma?"

"I don't know about Cynarra," Martha began, watching closely the work of the emergency medical technicians. "But Joshua seems to be suffering from exhaustion."

Missy was trembling uncontrollably. "Tired? He's just tired. But you were giving him CPR..."

Martha ducked back into the room and grabbed the blanket that Missy had discarded earlier. She wrapped it gently around her granddaughter and folded her in for a hug at the same time.

But Missy was still waiting for Martha's answer.

What was wrong with Joshua?

Martha said, "It's like when people get lost in the bush and they panic and start running around in circles..."

"But Joshua wouldn't panic," Missy protested.

Martha put an arm around her. "No, he wouldn't, honey. But it's kind of the same thing. If he had stopped to rest..."

Missy followed her gaze as she looked down at Cynarra. One of the EMT's was examining the deep wound on the little girl's leg; another was inserting an IV into her arm.

They'd stopped giving Joshua CPR.

The two technicians had rocked back on their heels and were looking down at him... just looking...

Missy pulled away from Martha and rushed forward.

"Joshua!" she sobbed.

A calm voice—Dan's calm voice—spoke close to her ear. "He's okay. He's breathing on his own now. We're just observing him."

Joshua's eyes were still closed. An oxygen mask was over his nose and mouth. An IV was in his arm. Missy watched his chest rise and fall.

She crumpled forward, weeping.

"He's going to be okay," Dan said again. "Now, I just need to ask you a few questions…"

Missy looked up and tried to focus on his face through the veil of tears.

"Is he on any heart medication?" Dan asked.

"No," Missy replied in a surprised voice. "He's only twenty-four!"

"So, no history of any heart problems?"

Missy shook her head. "My grandmother said that he might be suffering from exhaustion."

Dan nodded but didn't comment further.

Missy heard Cynarra cry out and turned to see them loading her onto a stretcher. She saw Martha take the little girl's hand and speak comforting words to her.

"We'll need their health cards," Dan said as they prepared to load Joshua onto a stretcher as well.

Missy hurried back into the lodge, knowing exactly where the envelope containing Cynarra's papers was since they'd had it out when she'd first gone missing and they'd contacted the Crisis Response Team.

On the way, she grabbed her handbag, which contained the health card that she shared with Joshua. If they went out of province, there might be some billing issues but that was the least of her worries now.

When Missy arrived back, she declared, "I'm going with you."

"It will depend if there's room or not," Martha advised.

"There'll be room," Dan said.

And there was.

They had secured the two stretchers each along one side of the airplane, Joshua and Cynarra's heads towards the front of the plane where three seats were located behind the pilot and copilot. Missy was thankful to be given the middle seat so that she could reach out and hold the hands of both Joshua and Cynarra. Dan was on the seat nearest to Joshua and the other EMT, a woman, was near Cynarra.

As the plane ascended, Missy felt, for the first time since Joshua had appeared on the patio with Cynarra in his arms, that she could finally relax a little. Joshua and Cynarra were being well taken care of and they were headed for a hospital and further medical treatment.

"Thank you," she spoke shyly, turning towards Dan first but including the other EMT as well. Her name was Larissa, according to her badge.

"Don't mention it," Dan said.

Larissa gave her a warm smile. "They're doing fine. Both of them."

Tears of relief filled Missy's eyes. And her heart soared with gratitude. "Thank you, Lord," she whispered.

Though Joshua remained still and silent, only the reassuring monitors indicating that all was well, Cynarra was now awake and alert. They'd started her on an IV right away and she'd been given an antibiotic and some pain medication. They'd decided though, not to disturb the bandages until they got her to a hospital. At least the bleeding seemed to have stopped. Her blood pressure was low but not dropping any further. They'd given her some sips of water and Cynarra was able to talk to them, though her voice was still weak.

As they flew on towards the hospital, Cynarra told them all about the bear that had chased her up a tree.

"He wanted my ham sandwiches," she said and added thoughtfully, "I would have shared."

Dan and Larissa both laughed but Missy only smiled. "How did you get away?" she asked.

Cynarra cast glowing eyes towards Joshua and her voice was filled with awe. "He fought the bear for me," she declared. "He hit it really hard on the nose and it ran away."

Larissa raised her eyes to meet Missy's, her look one of incredulity but Missy had no doubts about Cynarra's story. She smiled proudly. "You have a very brave uncle," she said.

"He wants to be my new daddy!" Cynarra exclaimed. "He's going to take care of me forever and ever."

Missy smiled. *Or at least until you're all grown up…*

"He's going to teach me to swim and to canoe—in his special favorite canoe. And at Christmas, there's always a big party…"

The little girl's voice trailed off. Her eyes closed.

She struggled to open them again. There was more she wanted to tell them. "He said—he would—protect me—with his life."

Missy smoothed back the wild, frizzy hair. When all this was over, she would buy Cynarra some nicely scented hair gel and maybe get some of the split ends trimmed off.

"It's okay, honey," she said softly, still stroking her hair. "We can talk later. You just go to sleep now."

"I want to see a loon…" Cynarra mumbled. "They have red beady eyes…"

Missy smiled then tears filled her eyes. "Joshua must have talked to her the whole way, to keep her spirits up."

Larissa nodded. "It may well have saved her life. There would have been more bleeding if she'd been upset and moving around a lot."

"He carried her the whole way," Missy said, feeling some of the awe that she'd heard in Cynarra's voice. Joshua *had* saved the little girl's life—and almost lost his own in the process.

Missy turned back towards her husband.

He was beginning to move restlessly.

Suddenly, his whole body jerked and his face contorted with pain.

Missy felt panic rising up in her. What was happening?

Dan was systematically checking all the monitors, trying to ascertain the problem, and Larissa was busy trying to reassure Cynarra who was struggling to get up off her stretcher. Everyone seemed to be talking at once, Joshua was still writhing in pain, and Missy couldn't at first hear what the little girl was trying to tell them.

But even when she did hear her, it didn't make sense.

"Massage and hot compresses!"

Was the little girl delirious? Maybe a fever had set in...

As Missy turned back towards Joshua, Cynarra grabbed her arm, her voice rising in desperation. "He needs massage and hot compresses. What's the matter with all of you?"

"Keep her still," Dan ordered. "She can't afford any more blood loss."

But Missy knew how determined Cynarra could be. "Let me take her," she said. Then without waiting for an answer, she released the strap holding Cynarra to the stretcher and began to ease her over onto her lap.

Protesting loudly, Larissa nonetheless was forced to quickly swing the IV pole around and reposition the monitors.

Cynarra was barely on Missy's lap when she leaned forward and lifted the cover off Joshua's legs. Everyone watched in surprise as the little girl began to massage the obviously locked muscles in the back of his right leg.

Dan finally caught his breath enough to say. "That's okay, honey. We'll take over now."

"How did she know?" Larissa asked in a strained voice.

"How far did he walk?" Dan asked.

Cynarra leaned wearily back into Missy's arms, glad to be relieved of her task. Missy tried to answer Dan's question first. "I'm not sure exactly. He left yesterday at about three in the afternoon and he just got back. If he was walking the whole time…"

"Hot compresses…" Cynarra murmured.

"How did she know?" Larissa asked again.

"She nursed her father," Missy replied. "He must have had leg cramps too."

"Drug side effects," Cynarra confirmed.

"You can't be serious! She's just a little child. What kind of father—"

Larissa's voice broke off as she saw the angry looks from both Missy and Cynarra.

"Hot compresses," Cynarra reminded them.

But the massage was already having an effect. Joshua was lying relaxed and still again.

Cynarra looked up at Missy. "Don't let them forget," she said in a weak, barely audible voice. Then her eyes drifted shut again.

"A rather precocious child," Dan commented dryly.

"A very capable and intelligent young lady," Missy corrected. "And very brave and beautiful, too."

She heard Cynarra give a small sigh and relax a little more into her arms. And Missy knew she'd said the right thing.

Missy held her for the rest of the flight and only with great reluctance placed her back on the stretcher for the airplane's descent.

Missy followed the stretchers into the emergency room where two teams of medical personnel converged upon them.

She wanted to ask questions and she wanted to be able to see what they were doing to both Joshua and Cynarra but Missy stood back as she was instructed, thankful that they hadn't barred her from the room altogether.

Joshua looked even paler in the bright lights of the emergency room. And he was lying so still...

Missy longed to be closer to him but everyone seemed so busy. Machines were beeping and humming and nurses were scurrying here and there, bringing more equipment and supplies. Doctors barked out orders and a curtain was whisked around Cynarra's bed shutting her off from view.

Missy heard the little girl begin to cry and a moment later, the curtain was pulled back again.

"Are you the child's mother?" an authoritative voice in green scrubs asked.

But the simple question had no simple answer. Joshua and she were planning to assume care of Cynarra and eventually adopt her. But what was she now? A foster mom? A guardian?

"Her aunt..." Missy suddenly remembered. "I'm her aunt."

The man eyed her critically. And Missy felt incredibly stupid. But Cynarra, turned over on her stomach so her leg could more easily be worked on, had stopped crying the moment that Missy had returned to the head of the bed.

"Whoever you are," the man said curtly, "stay right there where she can see you. She'll be out in a few minutes and then you can go."

"No!" Cynarra cried out. "Don't leave me!"

"Shh, it's okay, honey. I won't leave you. I'll stay right here."

Another man in green scrubs pulled up a stool and sat down beside her. He smiled and stretched out his hand in greeting. "My name is Dr. Worell; I'm the anesthesiologist."

Missy shook his hand and introduced herself.

Dr. Worell stood up again and pushed the stool towards her. "Here you sit down. I can just as easily stand."

Missy sank gratefully down on the stool, still keeping a firm hold of Cynarra's hand and maintaining eye contact with her.

"You have a very brave little girl here," Dr. Worell said.

Missy smiled at Cynarra. "Yes, I know."

As she spoke the words, Cynarra's eyes drifted shut.

"She's out," Dr. Worell said. "We shouldn't have to keep her under long…"

Missy focused her attention back on Joshua. The doctor attending him caught her eye and walked over. "Mrs. Quill?" he asked.

"Yes?" she replied, unable to keep the anxiety out of her voice.

"Your husband is in stable condition," he began.

"But why isn't he awake yet?" she asked fretfully.

"We've given him a sedative," the doctor replied. "What he needs most right now is to rest."

A sob caught in her throat and her voice broke as she asked, "What—what's wrong with him?"

The doctor took a step back. "Perhaps we could talk over here," he suggested.

"No!" Missy declared. "I promised I would stay with her."

"I'll call you the moment we start to bring her back," the anesthesiologist promised.

Missy reluctantly released Cynarra's hand and followed Joshua's doctor as he took a few more steps away from where they were still working on Cynarra's leg wound.

"Dr. Phillips," he introduced himself. "I'm a cardiologist."

"What's wrong with Joshua?" Missy asked again.

But instead of answering her, Dr. Phillips had questions of his own.

"Is he on any heart medication?"

"No," Missy replied.

"So, no history of any heart problems?"

"No. Please tell me what happened," Missy begged. "My grandmother is a nurse and she thinks he was suffering from exhaustion."

The cardiologist nodded sagely. "Mrs. Quill, your husband has had a heart attack, likely, as your grandmother suggested, brought on by overexertion. It is unusual for someone so young to have a heart attack even in these circumstances but it is not unknown. There may be an underlying condition that we are unaware of at this time."

Dr. Phillips gently squeezed her arm. "Try not to worry, Mrs. Quill. Your husband is doing just fine. At this point, there is no reason to not expect an excellent recovery."

Missy thanked him and took her place again beside Cynarra, her mind whirling with the news. A heart attack—it was what had killed her grandfather. It was what had almost killed her husband.

What underlying condition could Joshua possibly have and how would the discovery of this change their lives? Would he ever be able to resume leadership of their youth program? Perhaps it would be best if they just focused on their family for a while. Cynarra would need time to grieve and time to heal. And Joshua would need time to grieve and time to heal as well.

Chapter 11

Joshua felt as if he were covered with a heavy lead blanket. Even moving his fingers just a little seemed to require more strength than he possessed.

His eyelids, too, seemed weighted and it took a huge act of his will to open his eyes. And his only reward for all that effort was an endless view of white ceiling tiles.

He couldn't seem to remember where he was or why he was there.

If he could maybe turn his head just a little…

Pain shot through his neck and shoulder and down into his arm.

Joshua waited a moment for the worst of it to pass.

His eyes had involuntarily squeezed shut when the pain had rocketed through his shoulder. He forced his eyelids open again, intent on surveying at least some other part of the room besides the ceiling.

He saw Missy asleep in a chair. He tried to call her name. But though his lips moved, no sound came out.

There was something over his mouth and nose. If he could pull it off…

But he could barely lift his hand… pushing against the lead blanket…

It had to be a dream.

But it wasn't like the nightmares he usually had. In those, he couldn't move at all. No, he wasn't paralyzed by fear... He could move his hand a little. He had turned his head.

He tried to call her name again. *Nothing!*

"Hey, you're finally awake!"

Cynarra!

Cynarra... She was okay!

Joshua began the slow process of moving his head again. Pain shot through his other shoulder and arm this time and Joshua closed his eyes against it. Then he slowly, carefully expelled his held breath and forced open his eyelids.

Cynarra's little face appeared.

She was okay! He'd been so afraid that he wouldn't get her out of the bush on time—or at all. But he must have made it. She was here. He was here.

He tried to speak to ask her how she was. But his throat burned and his mouth was as dry as cotton.

"I'll call the nurse for you," Cynarra said.

She was sitting up in a bed beside his, her bandaged leg propped up on pillows. Joshua watched as she pressed the call switch.

He felt his eyelids grow heavy again...

As from a great distance, Joshua heard voices in the room.

A man's voice, kind and elderly: "He's doing just fine, Mrs. Quill. No need to worry."

"But shouldn't he be awake by now?" Missy asked.

"What he mostly needs right now is a lot of rest."

"But it's been almost twenty-four hours!" Missy protested.

"No, Mommy, he was awake while you were asleep," Cynarra interjected.

Mommy? Joshua forced his eyes open and carefully began to turn his head towards his wife and his future adopted daughter. He didn't want to miss another moment in their lives.

"Ah, looks like you're going to have your chance to talk to him after all," the man's voice sounded again from near the end of his bed. "Just don't tire him out now."

Missy bent over him and wrapped her arms around his neck. "Oh, Josh," she said in a tear-filled voice, "I was so worried about you."

He tried to put his arms around her but found he couldn't move them at all. At least, he assured himself, he could feel the warmth of her embrace and her wet tears on his face and her soft kisses.

"I was so afraid," she whispered. "So afraid…"

He tried to reassure her that he was okay now but when he tried to speak, no sound came out of his mouth!

For an awful moment, Joshua thought he might be dreaming.

She must have seen him moving his lips and the panic in his eyes when he couldn't make a sound. Her voice was soothing and full of reassurance as she told him, "Your throat is probably dry. I'll ask the nurse if you can have some water."

"I'll press the button," Cynarra said. "But this time you stay awake until she gets here, okay Daddy?"

Joshua looked past Missy to where Cynarra sat in a wheelchair and felt his heart burst with joy. It didn't matter that he couldn't move his arms or use his voice. This wonderful little girl was going to be in his heart and life now. He smiled at her and received a huge grin in return.

He didn't know when she'd come to the decision to call Missy and he, Mommy and Daddy but he remembered that sometime during that long trip back when he'd talked to her about her future at Rabbit Lake and the things they would all do together, Joshua had told her that she could call Missy and he, Mommy and Daddy if and when she was ready to.

It was so frustrating not having a voice! There were so many important things he wanted to talk to her about. On the long walk back, his conversation had all been one-sided. Now, she and Missy could talk but he couldn't.

A woman with a pastel floral print top arrived. Missy asked her about water and she came back a moment later with a blue plastic jug and a glass and straw.

She held the glass and straw for him and Joshua took a small sip.

But the water seemed to catch in his throat, which in turn made him cough. And suddenly, everything hurt from head to toe.

A cramp was starting in the calf of his left leg. And he couldn't speak to tell them!

"Left leg!" Cynarra's voice rang out as a command.

And suddenly, there was blessed heat wrapping around his leg, easing the cramp out of his muscle.

Joshua looked over in wonder at the little girl who was watching him intently now. "Is it better?" she asked.

Joshua nodded.

Missy smiled at the obvious surprise on his face. "It's part of the reason she won't leave you," Missy said. "She doesn't seem to trust anyone else with your care. They tried her in a room on the pediatric ward but she got so upset, they finally moved her in here."

Joshua raised his eyebrows questioningly towards Cynarra. She smiled serenely back at him.

Missy glanced over at the little girl and shook her head, a mixture of exasperation and pride on her face, as she continued. "It was actually quite a battle. She threatened to pull out all her stitches. The doctor threatened to sedate her..."

There was someone else in the room now. She had a white coat and an air of authority—his doctor? No, she was leaning over Cynarra—she must be her doctor.

"I just need to take a quick look at your stitches," the woman said, lifting up Cynarra's leg and peeling back the dressing. "Yes, they look fine…"

They didn't look fine to Joshua! From where he was lying, he had a clear view of the swollen and bruised area around the angry, red line of stitches. He tried to say something but again was frustrated in his attempts to communicate.

Joshua looked over at Missy but she was listening to the doctor who was saying to Cynarra, "You're healing up quite nicely. I'll be in again tomorrow to check on you." And with a smile, she was gone.

Joshua wanted to ask Cynarra if it hurt. It looked as if it must but maybe they were giving her enough pain medication… He tried to speak and this time, the nurse must have noticed because she put a pen in his hand and slid a piece of paper under it.

But Joshua had a further shock. He was too weak to write anything!

He couldn't press hard enough with the pen. He couldn't move his hand over the paper. The pen fell and he couldn't pick it up again. He couldn't even lift his head to see where it had fallen.

His frustration must have been obvious. Missy took his hand in hers, and the nurse patted him on the arm and said, "Your strength will come back. Don't you worry. You're making an amazing recovery."

An amazing recovery? *This* was an amazing recovery?

"Yes, you are," the nurse confirmed. "And most of the credit for that goes to your two faithful helpers here. Neither one of them has left your side for more than a few minutes since you arrived. And our little Ms. Dr. Quill here is the tyrant of the ward. She makes sure that you have everything you need—and then some!"

Joshua felt overwhelmed with love and gratitude as he exchanged smiles with the seven year old "Dr. Quill." Her fierce loyalty left him feeling humble and at the same time intensely proud of her.

"You have quite the family, Mr. Quill!" the nurse said in parting. "Hurry and get well so we can send you all home again."

Yes, Joshua thought, as he smiled over at Missy and Cynarra, he did have a wonderful family! And that's what they were now—no longer just a couple, but a family.

He tried to squeeze Missy's hand but he wondered if she would even notice his feeble effort.

But she had noticed. He felt her squeeze his hand in return.

"I don't know if you remember me telling you what happened and where you are?" Missy asked.

Joshua shook his head slightly. Even that took an effort! And a stab of pain shot through his neck and down into his right shoulder when he moved his head even a little.

"Does it still hurt to move?" Missy asked, her voice filled with concern.

Joshua only blinked his eyes this time.

"The doctor said that you had muscle spasms because of overexertion," Missy explained.

"Because of carrying me for so long," Cynarra added.

He could hear the worry in her voice and wanted to tell her it was okay; that he would gladly have walked twice that distance for her. But he could only hope that his smile reassured her.

"You seemed to wake up a little bit sometimes," Missy continued. "I talked to you and it seemed to calm you. But maybe you don't remember the things that I said…?"

Joshua mouthed the word "No" hoping she would understand.

"You're in the hospital in Thunder Bay," Missy began to carefully explain. We traveled together in an air ambulance yesterday morning—" Her voice broke and tears filled her eyes once more as she said, "I was so afraid, Josh. I was so afraid. Grandma was doing CPR on you and—" Missy couldn't speak anymore. She was crying.

And there was nothing he could do…

He couldn't even talk to her. And he wanted to put his arms around her…

"Hey now," a voice boomed, "you're not supposed to be tiring our patient."

Joshua looked up to see a large man almost filling the doorway. He wore wire-framed glasses set low on his nose. His voice was filled with authority and it seemed familiar to Joshua somehow.

"He needs rest. Perhaps you two ladies could take a break—maybe go down to the cafeteria." It could have been a suggestion but it wasn't. It was an order, plain and simple.

A nurse had followed in his wake. He turned to her. "Perhaps you could go down with them."

Joshua was grateful that she was there and available to accompany Missy and Cynarra. Maybe Missy could talk to her. And the nurse could talk back!

Missy wasn't ready to leave yet, though. "Dr. Phillips, why can't Joshua move—or even talk?"

The doctor seemed slightly annoyed that his order had not been immediately obeyed. He didn't reply to her but turned toward Joshua. He shone a flashlight down his throat and felt the sides of his neck. Then he rocked back on his heels. "Went for a long walk, did you?"

Joshua grinned wryly.

I guess you could say that.

"Talked as you walked?"

Joshua forgot that nodding his head would hurt so much.

The doctor looked over the rim of his glasses. "Carried a bit of a load?"

She wasn't heavy!

"Our bodies do have limitations." The doctor sighed. "A physiotherapist will be in to see you later. Your voice should return in a day or two. Get some rest." He turned meaningfully towards Missy and Cynarra.

As the door closed behind them, Joshua had to smile.

He suddenly felt insanely, ridiculously happy.

Missy would be okay after she'd had a chance to talk to someone. Maybe she could even call and talk to Martha. He'd have his voice back in a day or two and he'd tell her how much he loved her.

Cynarra was alive and healing well. And he was anxious to also tell her how much he loved her.

Chapter 12

HER GRANDMA WAS IN THE waiting room when Missy emerged from the Intensive Care Unit. So was that lawyer fellow that had talked to Joshua about Bryan's affairs. Missy felt as if she was too tired to talk to any lawyer. But it seemed as if she didn't have a choice.

"We met briefly," he said. "Robin Finley."

Missy shook his extended hand in greeting.

"I have some more papers for you and your husband," he said. "I called your number and they said that you were here. Your grandmother told me everything that happened."

Missy sank into the sofa beside Martha.

Robin had risen to speak to her but took a seat when Missy did, the four of them forming a rough circle with Cynarra's wheelchair between their sofa and the lawyer's chair.

He turned to Cynarra. "I'm sorry about your father," he said. "And I have something for you, from him."

Tears were in Cynarra's eyes as she whispered, "You do?"

Robin smiled gently. "It's a video. He'd been working on it a long time. He made it just for you but if you'd like some of your new family to watch it with you, that would probably be okay too."

Cynarra looked up at Missy. "Could we?"

"I can arrange for a place where you and your husband can watch it with her if you'd like to—perhaps even this afternoon," the lawyer suggested.

Her husband... Missy hesitated. "Joshua..."

"How is he, dear?" Martha quickly interjected. "The nurse told us he was awake now."

Missy's heart leapt with joy. "Yes, he's so much better, Grandma." Some of her joy faded as she continued, "He's still really weak though and he can't talk at all."

"He carried me a really long way... and he talked all the time... the whole way," Cynarra said in a worried voice.

"It could be that he has laryngitis," Martha suggested.

"He talked all the time," Cynarra said, her lower lip beginning to quiver.

Three people reached out to her at the same time, all anxious to reassure the little girl.

"I'm sure he'll be fine in a day or two," Martha said.

"It wasn't your fault," Robin said.

"Joshua loves you," Missy said.

Cynarra's eyes grew wide. "He does?"

Like an echo in stereo, both Martha and Robin asked, "He does?"

Missy and Cynarra exchanged a smile, which turned into a giggle.

"Come 'ere," Missy said, drawing the little girl into her arms. "You're too far away."

Cynarra snuggled close, resting her head on Missy's shoulders, suddenly oblivious to the other two. "Does he really love me, Mommy, does he?"

"Yes, pumpkin, he really loves you. And I really love you, too." Missy snuggled down into her arms and promptly fell asleep!

"Wow, that was quick!" Robin said in a hushed voice.

Missy nodded. "She hasn't slept much in the last couple of days. The pain medication didn't seem to have a sedative effect on her. She's been talking almost non-stop to me, telling me in great detail all the things that Joshua told her on their walk home. But this time through, she was able to ask me all the questions she had wanted to ask Joshua."

Robin grinned. "Guess you'll be glad to have her asleep for a while."

Missy nodded. But truthfully, she hadn't minded all of Cynarra's constant chatter. It had helped to distract Missy's mind from the uncertainty of Joshua's condition.

But it was as if now that they both knew that he was going to be okay, they both could sleep. Missy felt as if she could quite possibly sleep for a day or two or maybe a whole week!

Robin offered to carry Cynarra to her room, and after a nod of agreement from Missy, gently lifted Cynarra out of her arms. Martha gave Missy a hug in farewell and told her that she would be praying for her.

The little girl didn't wake up at all as Missy got them buzzed back through into the Intensive Care Unit. Joshua seemed to be asleep too. Missy unfolded Cynarra's cot and Robin set her down on it. Missy tucked her in, smoothed back her hair and kissed her gently on the cheek.

When she looked up again, she was surprised to see that both Joshua and Robin had been watching her and Cynarra.

Robin's voice was usually smooth and professional but it sounded deep and gravelly when he said to Joshua, "You're a lucky man."

Joshua, unable to reply, nodded in acknowledgement and Robin turned to go.

"The video…" Missy remembered.

Robin flipped a business card out of the breast pocket of his suit jacket. "Whenever you're ready," he said. "I'll stop by again this evening—seven o'clock in the waiting room. Don't hesitate to call if there's anything I can do. And just let me know whenever you're ready for the video." He was silent for a moment before continuing in a less business-like tone. "You would have liked Bryan. He was a remarkable man in so many ways. He'd risen above his past. He'd made something out of his life. People admired him. You'll understand when you see the video." Robin looked full at Joshua. "He's maybe not the person whom you remember."

Joshua blinked in acknowledgement and smiled fragilely.

Robin turned to Missy. "There are some papers to be signed, also, regarding Cynarra. And there are boxes of their stuff that will need to be sorted through. But there's no hurry for any of that. The most important thing now is that Cynarra and Joshua get completely well again."

Robin handed Missy his business card and smiled sardonically. "I have a very limited, but very rich, clientele. I answer phone calls at just about any hour of the day or night—within reason of course—I do sleep occasionally."

Missy was too surprised to say anything. Did he expect them to be calling him on a regular basis? What possible reason could they have for that?

As if in answer to her unspoken question, Robin waved his hand toward Cynarra's cot. "She can afford a private room, you know."

"She—she wants to be with him—with Joshua," Missy said, stumbling over her words, feeling her face flush in embarrassment.

"And that's fine," the lawyer quickly amended.

Missy raised her chin and said, "We can afford a private room for her, too."

Robin said in a soothing tone, "I know that Cynarra will be well taken care of by both of you." He smiled kindly at Missy and let his eyes rest on the sleeping Cynarra for a moment before turning to Joshua and saying once again, "You're a very lucky man." And with that, he was gone.

"And I'm a very lucky woman," Missy said softly as she smoothed back Joshua's hair and kissed his cheek as she had Cynarra's.

Joshua smiled at her, conveying all the love he couldn't communicate any other way.

Missy was just glad to have him back again. She'd come so close—*so close!*—to losing him.

Joshua motioned with his eyes and lips towards her cot, still folded up on the other side of his bed. He looked concerned—for her.

"You're right," Missy said with a sigh. "I am tired. And I should sleep while little Miss Chatterbox is sleeping."

Joshua's eyebrows rose in a question.

Missy grinned and explained. "I think I heard almost every single thing that you said to Cynarra on the trip home. It's actually quite a wonder that *she* doesn't have laryngitis as well!"

Joshua carefully moved his head so that he could look at Cynarra. He smiled lovingly at her before turning back to his wife and grinning broadly.

"Yeah," Missy spoke for him, "she's a great kid."

Missy had gone out to the nurses' station and let them know that they would all be trying to sleep for a while. Even so, she was surprised when she next looked at her watch and found that it was almost 7:30 PM! She had slept for almost eight hours straight!

She got quietly up off the bed, noted that Joshua and Cynarra were still asleep, and tiptoed out of the room.

Robin was waiting for her and Martha was back again as well.

"Everyone's sleeping," she told Robin apologetically.

"That's just what's needed right now," Martha said, giving her a big hug.

Robin agreed. "We'll come back in the morning."

"Call me if there's anything you need," Martha added.

Missy thanked them both, headed back into their room and was soon fast asleep once more.

They decided to move Joshua to the regular ward in the morning, and once again, the hospital made an exception, allowing all three of them to share a room together.

The physiotherapist arrived and prescribed some range of motion exercises for Joshua. She helped him to sit on the edge of the bed for a few minutes and had advised him that he could probably try a short walk by that evening.

Joshua was still frustrated by how weak he felt but the "lead blanket" had been lifted and he was able to move around a bit without fear of his muscles seizing up.

He could speak in a strained whisper but his doctor had cautioned him not to. His voice would heal quicker if he rested it completely. And he was strong enough now that he could write out what he wanted to say.

Cynarra always seemed to be full of questions. Just then, she was asking Missy about life after death. The bigger question that Cynarra wanted to know, of course, was where her daddy was now.

Missy pulled her pocket Bible out of her handbag and began to show Cynarra some verses about heaven.

The inevitable question came. "Is my daddy in heaven?"

Missy lifted troubled eyes up to Joshua.

Joshua felt as if his heart was going to burst with joy as he nodded and mouthed the word, "Yes".

Joshua did believe with all his heart that, at that very moment, his brother, Bryan, was walking and talking with his new best friend, the Lord Jesus!

Tears filled Missy's eyes as she told Cynarra that her daddy was with Jesus now, that he was happy and safe and free from all pain.

Cynarra's smile lit up her face.

"Well, you folks sure are looking better today."

Robin Finley walked in carrying a briefcase, and wearing his usual dark blue suit and air of professionalism.

Cynarra smiled up at him. "My daddy's in heaven!" she declared.

Robin seemed a little uncomfortable with the idea. He smiled faintly at Cynarra and raised his eyebrows at Missy and her open Bible.

"You guys don't waste any time, do you?" he asked cryptically.

Missy and Joshua exchanged glances but it was Cynarra who spoke first. There was just a slight catch in her voice as she said, "I'm glad all the bad pain is gone and my daddy isn't sick anymore."

Robin nodded and his smile was genuine this time. "I am too," he said, bending down to give Cynarra a hug.

Robin had brought the video with him, and it was arranged that they would see it at two o'clock that afternoon. Missy, Joshua and Cynarra would watch it together first, and later they could decide if they wanted to use parts or all of it for a memorial service or if they just wanted to share it with individual family members.

Joshua wondered if anyone had got hold of Russell and Garby yet. He wrote the question out for Robin who said that he didn't know but would find out.

As the hour approached, Joshua felt a weight of depression settling over him. In spite of all that had happened, he still wasn't sure that he was ready to see this video of his brother's.

He knew he had to go through with it, for Cynarra's sake, but he didn't anticipate that it would be in any way easy or enjoyable.

Robin had arranged a private room, which looked as if it might be a doctor's lounge. There was a loveseat with reclining end seats and Joshua was made comfortable in a semi-reclining position. Cynarra and Missy sat beside him, both of them slim enough to fit together in the one seat. Cynarra had her injured leg propped up beside Joshua's.

Joshua gave Cynarra the remote so she could pause the video at any time if she wanted to. In some ways, Bryan was still very much a stranger to him and Joshua had no idea what would be on the video. He wished suddenly that he had looked at it first...

It had a professional feel to it right from the beginning and seemed more like a movie they would rent, rather than a home video. There was music in the background and the video clips of Cynarra were choreographed with a song that seemed to have been written especially for her. It had a beautiful haunting melody and the lyrics told of her life and of her daddy's love for her. "Your tiny fingers wrapped around mine and my heart was yours for all time..."

Joshua's eyes were as much on Cynarra as they were on the movie. She was smiling and even laughed once when there was a clip of her as a one-year-old smearing birthday cake all over herself.

It wasn't until Bryan's voice-over came that she became still and silent. "Cynarra," he said in a tender voice, "from the moment I first saw you, I knew I would love you till the day I died…"

Joshua took one of Cynarra's hands in his, and Missy took the other as the video continued.

There was a Christmas scene next. A younger, healthier Bryan was helping the toddler, Cynarra, to unwrap her gifts. There was Christmas music playing in the background and over that, Bryan's voice once more. "I wanted to give you all the things that I'd never had as a child. I wanted everything to be perfect."

The camera moved up the beautifully decorated tree and zoomed in on the angel at the top. "I never imagined that I might die and leave you alone." Bryan's voice broke as he continued, "I wish I could change that."

Tears were trickling down Cynarra's cheeks now.

Missy and Joshua exchanged glances and Missy leaned towards Cynarra. "Would you like to pause it, or keep going?" she asked.

With a stifled sob, Cynarra clicked the remote and moved to the security of Missy's lap, burying her face in her shoulder.

"Your daddy loved you," Missy said softly.

Cynarra pulled away a little. "He didn't want to go away—to heaven."

"Your daddy would have stayed with you if he could have," Missy assured her.

Cynarra nodded, snuggled into Missy's shoulder again and pressed "play" on the remote.

The next scene was of a laughing baby Cynarra walking unsteadily towards the camera. "You weren't only beautiful but you were smart too—and funny." Baby Cynarra started clapping her hands and laughing.

"You walked when you were ten months old and you were chattering away by the time you were a year. By fourteen months, there was a whole bunch of words that you could say. You loved books…"

A studious looking two year old was flipping pages on a book that looked almost as big as her!

"We read you stories all the time and of course, I always practiced my lines on you, my most appreciative audience."

There was a scene from one of Bryan's movies, which faded into a giggling Cynarra pointing at the camera and laughing.

That Bryan could laugh at himself was something that Joshua didn't know. A person had to have a lot of self-confidence to be able to laugh at themselves. Had Bryan felt confident as an actor… as a father… as a brother…?

He'd been so sure that Joshua would take Cynarra in. Did that show confidence in himself—or in Joshua?

"You were also very creative… and you liked to help."

There was a scene with Cynarra, who looked to be about three "helping" to paint part of what appeared to be a movie set.

"Everyone loved you," the voice of Bryan continued as one of the painters bent down beside Cynarra and drew a cartoon character for her, one that would have to be painted over before the day was done.

"You had to go to work with me sometimes. There were always lots of people ready and willing to entertain you…" A young man in a Mime costume was making a balloon animal for Cynarra as Bryan spoke.

"In the beginning, you spent a lot of time with Terry and, of course, we did things together as a family." A young Black man with dreads and a purple bandana was playing on a Djembe while a four or five-year-old Cynarra drummed away on a set of Toms beside him. Bryan came onto the scene with a microphone and was obviously singing karaoke to some background music. The music continued but the scene changed to a large swimming pool where the three of them were laughing and splashing each other. Terry grabbed Bryan and kissed him full on the mouth. Cynarra watched unconcerned then began laughing and splashing them both again. They broke apart, Bryan playfully splashing Cynarra again as Terry swam away.

"I thought we would always be together," Bryan said in a voice that still seemed to hold some bewilderment. The camera focused on Terry and went to slow motion as he swam away from the other two. "Terry was my first and only lover. I thought that we would be a family always. I thought that he loved me as much as I loved him."

Joshua reached for the remote. *He* needed a break this time.

What was he going to tell Cynarra about homosexuality?

Cynarra looked up at him. "I didn't like having two daddies," she said. She stared at the blank TV. "They were always fighting."

"Sometimes, husbands and wives fight, too," Missy said.

Joshua protested, almost forgetting that he shouldn't use his voice.

Missy just grinned and raised an eyebrow.

Well, maybe they did disagree once in a while…

Missy leaned over to kiss him lightly on the cheek.

Joshua smiled. It was okay to fight if you could kiss and make up later!

But Cynarra's thoughts were on a more serious note. "They got really mad at each other when they were fighting. And sometimes Terry would hurt Bryan. I called the police one time. Then Terry got really mad at me."

Joshua fumbled for his notepad and pen. "Did he hurt you?" he wrote.

Cynarra read the question and nodded without looking up.

White-hot anger rose up within him. "Never again!" Joshua scribbled furiously on the notepad.

Cynarra read the note and looked sadly up at him. "My daddy's dead," she said simply. "He's not going to fight with Terry anymore."

"No one! No one will ever hurt you again!" Joshua wrote in a firm hand.

Cynarra's smile began slowly but grew wider and her eyes shone as she declared. "You beat up a big monster bear for me!"

Joshua had hoped and prayed that she wouldn't have terrible nightmares about the experience. So far, it didn't seem to have affected her that way. Cynarra seemed almost proud of her story.

Joshua smiled at her. It was a great story. And Cynarra was a great kid.

Chapter 13

THEY CONTINUED TO WATCH the rest of the video after that. Bryan had interspersed some of his movie clips in with some home videos of Cynarra to make an entertaining story.

Joshua observed that Cynarra could read quite well at a very young age. She often had a script in her hand and corrected Bryan while he was rehearsing at home.

The video also revealed Bryan's deteriorating health. The pounds seemed to fall away and as Cynarra aged four years in the video, Bryan seemed to age forty.

Terry wasn't included in any of the pictures after the swimming pool, and Joshua didn't ask Cynarra any more questions about him.

A still photo of Bryan and Cynarra was the last image that appeared as the music faded off. Bryan's last words were spoken softly—"I love you, Cynarra."

The three of them sat silently watching the blank screen each with their own thoughts.

Suddenly, Bryan's voice came once again.

Joshua was surprised to hear his name spoken. No image appeared on the screen and it felt strange to hear Bryan speaking into the stillness of the room.

"Joshua, I hope you're watching this and I hope that means that you've decided to care for my daughter. This message is for you…"

Joshua quickly hit the remote. If his brother had a personal message for him, it might not be suitable for Cynarra to hear.

Missy lifted Cynarra back into her wheelchair and rose quickly to her feet. "We'll come back in a little while," she said.

Joshua nodded and mouthed the word, "Thank you." Cynarra was out of reach for a hug but Joshua mouthed and mimed the words, "I love you."

Cynarra blinked back tears as she said, "I love you, too."

When they were gone, Joshua reluctantly pressed the "play" button again.

Bryan's voice sliced through the silence of the room. "As you've seen in the video, she's had a good life for the most part. Though with my acting career and then with this… illness… well, it hasn't been exactly normal. She's never been to a regular school but she's had good tutors; she reads better than a lot of kids twice her age, and she knows basic math. Being around adults most of her life has probably made her more mature in some ways. Then too, she's had a lot of responsibility recently. Someone came to clean once a day and I had an arrangement with a near-by restaurant that delivered meals to us each day. We did try a few live-in helpers but it wasn't a great success. Things seemed to work better with just the two of us."

Joshua thought about all the things that he had talked to Cynarra about on their walk home. Missy had said that Cynarra had told her all about them. Joshua once again silently vowed that he would bring some fun into this little girl's life. They would go canoeing and swimming and camping, and in the winter it would be Winter

Carnival time with contests and prizes and hockey games. And she would go to school too and have friends her own age over to play...

"I know you won't approve of all that I've done," Bryan's voice broke into his thoughts. "Maybe you won't approve of *anything* that I've done. But I hope that you will allow Cynarra to have her good memories of our brief life together. I hope that you will allow her to view this video when she wants to. If there is one thing in my life that I want to be remembered for, it isn't my success in films but my success as a father."

Thinking of what he knew of Cynarra so far, Joshua had to admit that perhaps Bryan was right—he had been successful as a father.

"There's a lot of money," Bryan continued. "I've left it all for Cynarra. You and Robin are trustees until she gets to be eighteen. If there's anything that she needs... But you will likely not want to take anything from me and I've heard you're independently wealthy."

Joshua's jaw tightened. He'd been given a ministry—and the money to do it with. Bryan made it sound as if Joshua was going to buy a yacht and sail to the Bahamas!

"If you're watching this," Bryan's voice continued, "I hope you and I have had a chance to talk. This illness is so unpredictable. I hope I've had a chance to tell you that I'm sorry for what happened when we were young. To be quite honest with you, I'm not sure that I would have made the effort to reconcile if it hadn't been for Cynarra. It was a lot easier just to forget I had a family back in Rabbit Lake. Now... Now it seems important. I know you will take care of Cynarra because she is your niece. I also heard that you got religion and I'm hoping that will help you to overlook the fact that she is my daughter."

Joshua felt shame wash over him. It had taken a lot to soften his heart towards Bryan's daughter. He hadn't immediately demonstrated the love of Jesus to her.

Brian's voice continued. "I hope that you will come to love her as I do and that your wife will accept her too. I hear you married an African-American woman. Perhaps she will help Cynarra to deal with the prejudice she may encounter at Rabbit Lake and elsewhere throughout her life. We have certainly experienced our fair share of it so far.

"Well brother, I guess it's goodbye. Cynarra, if you're still there, I—I just wish things could be different. Don't—don't ever forget that Daddy loves you. I'll always love you, baby, always…"

Bryan's voice trailed off and was gone.

Joshua felt an overwhelming sadness and a weariness that was bone deep. His brother was gone—gone forever.

No, someday they would meet again. And there would be nothing between them anymore. There would be no sickness or sadness or pain. Just peace and joy and love and that—*that* would be forever.

THE DOCTORS WERE PLEASED with Joshua's and Cynarra's recovery and decided to release them both the following day. It helped a lot that Martha would be on hand to take care of them. Though it had been many years now since she had renewed her license, she had been a well-trained and experienced nurse in her time.

Both Joshua and Cynarra were at the stage of using walkers to get around and they had already taken several walks together up and down the hallway of the hospital.

The trip home on the plane tired them both and they spent the rest of the day relaxing by the fire and receiving visits from family and friends.

Cynarra got to meet her young cousin, Keiron, and they hit it off right away. Starla, also her cousin, was warmly accepting of her. And Cynarra was thrilled to meet Starla's daughter, Karissa, who was one and a half years old.

Because people hadn't had a chance to see them in the hospital, they brought get-well gifts and cards now. Cynarra, in particular, was showered with stuffed animals, candy, books and games.

In the evening, when Cynarra was up in bed, Charles, Martha and Keegan lingered by the fireplace with Joshua and Missy, and the conversation grew more serious.

"I've been fielding a few calls," Charles said. "There are one or two decisions to be made. Maybe I could discuss them with you, Joshua…"

Keegan leaned forward and added, "I should probably tell you that Michael and Rosalee have been packing their stuff. They're planning to leave sometime this weekend."

Joshua nodded solemnly. It was what he had expected. But still it saddened him. It was Wednesday evening. If they were planning to leave on the weekend, he might only have a day or two to talk to them. It didn't seem right to leave things as they were with Michael.

He wished they weren't leaving—but if they were unhappy with how he was running things…

Suddenly, he remembered… "You wanted to talk to me, too!" Joshua couldn't keep the anxiety from his voice as he met Keegan's eyes.

Keegan grinned. "Don't worry. I'm not going anywhere. I was actually wanting to talk to you about Michael—and the camp staff in general. I was thinking that we just need more time together as a team before we start with another group of kids. I've been feeling

Michael's growing anxiety for a while now—and it might have been better if we could have talked about it earlier."

"Yes," Joshua said with a deep sigh. "I haven't been handling things too well."

"You've been doing just fine," Charles quickly interjected. "Tom would be proud of you."

"Yes, he would," Martha said.

Keegan nodded and Missy squeezed his hand.

Joshua smiled his thanks, feeling humbled and grateful for their kind words and their ongoing support.

Charles said, "There was a guy from the Department of Northern Development and Mines that stopped by yesterday. He said that he'd talked to you last week about reclamation of the old mine site."

Joshua sighed. "Yes…"

"They'd just like to see things get started sometime this summer. I told him about your heart attack and also that you'd just lost your brother. They're willing to extend the grace period a bit—give you some time."

"Thanks, Charles," Joshua said, feeling a load being lifted off his shoulders.

"Your Aunt Yvonne…" Charles began.

Joshua tensed again. "Yes?"

But Charles only wanted to tell him that Yvonne was insisting that they have a community memorial service for Bryan, and Joshua was happy to comply with her wishes. Missy told Charles about the video that Bryan had made.

"How are you feeling?" Keegan asked Joshua when there was a lull in the conversation.

Joshua smiled. "Good!" he declared. Though his throat still hurt, he had his voice back, and his strength was slowly but surely returning.

"I was wondering if you would still like to have our support group meeting—maybe tomorrow evening. I could lead it if you like," Keegan volunteered.

"That'd be great!" Joshua exclaimed. "Thanks."

JOSHUA FELT EVEN STRONGER the next day but was still grateful that Keegan had volunteered to lead the support group.

There were seven members of the group who met each week for the seven-step program: Joshua and Missy; Keegan and his wife, Randi; Lewis and his wife, Starla; and Missy's sister, Jasmine.

It was the third week and Keegan read out the step for that week:

"STOP BLAMING YOURSELF FOR A CRIME YOU DID NOT COMMIT.

"God will not hold you responsible for another's sin against you. Satan is the one who would accuse you and make you feel at fault. God is just in all His dealings. You need to have His viewpoint on the matter.

"It is sad to see so many commit suicide because of false guilt.

"Put the shame where it belongs, on the abuser.

"It is not yours to carry."

Joshua knew there was still much he had to learn in this regard.

When it was his turn to share, Joshua told the others that he still struggled with feelings of responsibility for what his brothers had done to him because he had gone willingly the first few times to the old shack. His brothers had started off teasing and playful but the violence escalated with each subsequent visit to the cabin, and the physical and emotional wounds that were inflicted left scars that would remain with Joshua for the rest of his life.

"They were so much older than me," Joshua told the group. "But they were my brothers. I wanted them to like me." Joshua bowed his head. "I guess I'd have done anything that they wanted me to."

"My dad did the same thing to me at home but even with him, I didn't try to fight him off. Sometimes, it seemed as if he liked me a bit. He wasn't so mad at me when he was—"

"When he was sexually abusing you?" Keegan asked.

Joshua averted his eyes from everyone as he replied, "It was hard for me at the time to recognize it as abuse. I liked when he paid attention to me, especially when I was really young. Sometimes his teasing would get out of hand—and he'd hurt me. I don't think he meant to…"

"Joshua," Missy said in a gentle but firm voice, "what your father and brothers did to you was wrong."

Joshua turned and met her eyes, knowing but unable to fully take in the truth of her words. He had shared some of the details of the abuse with her—enough for her to understand a bit of what he'd gone through.

"And none of it was your fault," she said. "You were just a kid—and they were adults."

"You were only fourteen when you came here to live with Martha and Tom, weren't you?" Keegan asked.

Joshua nodded, forcing his mind back to the summer when both his sister and his father had taken their own lives. He'd never had a chance to reconcile with his father. And he'd never gotten past the shame and regret he felt over his sister's suicide.

"I wish there was some way I could have protected my sister," he said. "I was so wrapped up in my own problems. I was even doing drugs…"

"I was guilty of the same thing," Keegan said. "I actually led my brother into taking drugs with me." Keegan looked over at his brother, Lewis, as he continued. "I very much regret not being there for him the way that I should have been."

"But at least he's here to apologize to," Missy said, voicing Joshua's thoughts.

Keegan nodded. "Yes, that's true and his forgiveness means a lot to me."

Joshua watched the exchange between the two brothers and wished with all his heart that his sister Rebecca was still alive and that he could tell her how sorry he was.

Starla, usually so quiet in their meetings, said in a shy, quiet voice, "Sometimes we can't apologize to the person we hurt because they're no longer living but we can always go to God. We can confess our sins to Him and He will forgive us—it says so in the Bible."

Keegan smiled at his young sister-in-law. "That's right," he said. "If we do feel guilty for something that is truly our fault, then we can experience forgiveness from God. All we have to do is confess our sins, which means telling him what we did wrong."

"One of the good things about that," Missy added, "is that it forces us to spell out exactly what it is we did wrong. And maybe with that knowledge, we can recognize the things that were not our fault." She leaned towards her husband. "Joshua, I know how much you tried to protect your sister. Rebecca didn't take her life because you neglected her; she took her life because of the awful abuse that she was suffering from other family members—not from you."

Keegan nodded. "Ask the Lord to forgive you for the things that you know you did wrong—and *accept* that forgiveness! Then release all the rest of the blame and shame that others have put on you or that you have put on yourself. The Lord never meant for us to be carrying around such heavy weights of guilt. He came to set us free—to bring us joy."

Joshua remained silent a moment, letting the truth of their words sink deep into his heart. "I'd like to pray," he said, "here and now with all of you, if I may."

Missy, in the chair beside him, took his hand, and the other five members of the group gathered around, each of them laying a hand on his back or shoulder or arm. He felt their comfort and support as he prayed. "Dear Lord, I ask you right now to forgive me for not being there for my sister the way that I would have liked to have been. I ask you to forgive me for turning to drugs instead of turning to you or to other people who might have been able to help us. And I today accept your forgiveness and believe that you have completely and totally forgiven me and made me clean. I am releasing all of the shame and all of the guilt that does not belong to me. Please help me to walk in your freedom and in your love. In Jesus name, Amen."

As Joshua turned to receive a hug first from his wife and then from other members of the group, joy bubbled up from deep within, and a song of thanksgiving filled his heart.

KAITLYN HAD COME OVER TO THE lodge to babysit Karissa and Chance while their parents attended the meeting, and Cynarra had stayed up in the nursery with them as well. After everyone else was gone, Cynarra told Missy and Joshua how much she had enjoyed herself. "I'm going to be a babysitter when I grow up," she declared.

Joshua and Missy laughed, and Missy said, "It's good you're getting some practice now. I'll be needing your help when the baby comes."

Cynarra's eyes grew wide with delight. "Really?"

Missy gave her a big hug. "Really!"

Joshua put his arms around both of them, once again feeling unrestrained joy fill his heart. There would still be difficulties ahead, he knew, but together they would weather the storms of life—together as a family.

Author's Note

If you have been sexually abused, it is very important that you talk to someone you trust: a teacher or your pastor or youth counselor.

If you know of someone under the age of sixteen who is being sexually abused, it is against the law to not report it to the authorities: the police or a social agency.

If you have been sexually abused in the past, the first step on your journey of healing will be to acknowledge that it happened and that it is affecting you today. You need to look honestly at the problems in your life and be willing to accept the help and counsel of others.

To know Jesus is to know the Great Healer. The Bible says that God loves you. He loves you so much that He sent Jesus to pay the price for your sin (it's like somebody taking your jail sentence for you so you can go free). Speaking of Himself in John 10:10 and 11, Jesus said: "I came that they might have life, a great full life. I am the Good Shepherd. The Good Shepherd gives His life for the sheep."

Jesus gave His life for you. But the Good News is that He didn't stay dead. He came alive again after three days. The Bible says that He "swallowed up death in victory"! (Isaiah 25:8 and I Corinthians 15:54 KJV).

He only asks us to trust Him. A simple but often difficult decision for someone who has been betrayed by those whom they should have been able to trust. Though your earthly father may have hurt you, your Heavenly Father loves you and because He is perfect, His love for you is perfect.

Life here on earth may be difficult but it is a journey we all must take. There is Someone who wants to walk beside us. When we talk to God and tell Him of our troubles, He hears us and the Bible says that the Holy Spirit is there to comfort us. As you read more of the Bible, you will learn more about God and He will speak truth to your mind and to your heart.

The Lord bless you!

M. Dorene Meyer

dorene@dorenemeyer.com

Recommended Resources

1. The Bible—available in many versions. Find one that's easy for you to read.
2. Visit www.risingabove.ca—excellent site that will direct you towards resources, conferences in your area, and hope and healing.
3. Bordeleau, Rose-Aimee. *Breaking the Silence.* Raphah Worldwide Ministries, 2002. Also available from www.raphah.org.
4. Cefrey, Holly. *AIDS.* The Rosen Publishing Group, Inc. 2001
5. Draimin, Barbara Hermie. *Coping When a Parent has AIDS.* The Rosen Publishing Group, Inc. 1994.
6. Frank, Jan. *A Door of Hope.* Thomas Nelson Publishers, 1993.
7. Heitritter, Lynn and Jeanette Vought. *Helping Victims of Sexual Abuse.* Bethany House Publishers, 1989.
8. Jolly, Howard. *Hope for the Hurting.* Rising Above Counseling Agency, 1996.
9. Kubler-Ross, Elizabeth. *AIDS – The Ultimate Challenge.* Macmillan Publishing Company, 1987. Republished in 1997 by Simon & Shuster.
10. Poulin, Selma. *How to Counsel a Sexually Abused Person.* Rising Above Counseling Agency.

Questions for Group Discussion or Personal Reflection—Week Three

When a person has been sexually, physically or verbally abused as a child, they often grow up with very low self-esteem. They feel as if they somehow deserved the abuse they received as a child. This causes a feeling of shame that can last a lifetime.

Answer the following questions (regarding self-esteem):

1. What do I like about myself?

    - Mentally:

    - Emotionally:

    - Socially:

    - Spiritually:

    - Physically:

2. If I had the power to do so, what would I change about myself?

3. Who has, in my past, made me feel defective, inadequate, as if I didn't measure up? How did they do this?

4. Who has made me feel loved and worthwhile? How have they done this?

5. Are there things in my life that I have done wrong that I need to confess to others or to God? (Take a moment now to do this.)

6. Are there things in my life that I have been feeling guilty about that were not my fault? (List them here.)

7. Take a moment now to release to God the shame and the blame that you have carried. Realize that you are fully forgiven, clean and pure in God's sight. Rest in the sure knowledge of His love for you. You are His most precious child!

Acknowledgements

At this point in the series, I would like to take a moment to thank the people who have helped me in my writing journey.

To Selma Poulin, a Native Mental Clinician, board member of Rising Above Abuse Counselling Agency, and author of *How to Counsel a Sexually Abused Person*, thank you for reading these manuscripts in their embryonic stages and encouraging me to continue writing this series.

Thank you also to Lisa Holiday, editor extraordinaire! You continually challenge me to improve my writing skills and to think through the placement of each comma and the description of each character. You are amazing!

And I would have thrown in the towel many years ago without the loving support of my dear husband, John. Thank you for discussing with me the various topics, plots and characters in this series. Thank you for reading, critiquing and editing my manuscripts. Thank you for sharing this ministry in every way possible. Your encouragement and support mean everything to me!

And, last but not least, my deepest gratitude to you, my readers. Thank you for joining me on this incredible journey!